After the Pain
(Latter Rain Series: Book 1)

I0556589

Adrienne Thompson

Pink Cashmere Publishing

Arkansas, USA

Cover art by AA Thompson (thompson9699@gmail.com)

Printed in the United States of America

First Printing 2016

Copyright © 2016 Adrienne Thompson

ISBN: 0-9971461-3-3

ISBN-13: 978-0-9971461-3-4

"See! The winter is past; the rains are over and gone."

Song of Songs 2:11 NIV

Soundtrack:

"Rain" *SWV*

"Dark Times" *The Weeknd featuring Ed Sheeran*

"Zoom" *The Commodores*

"Cruisin'" *Smokey Robinson*

"On My Own" *Patti LaBelle featuring Michael McDonald*

"Papillion" *Chaka Khan*

"In the Morning" *Ledisi*

"Amorous" *Jesse Boykins III*

"A Long Walk" *Jill Scott*

"Being with You" *Smokey Robinson*

"Could it be I'm Falling in Love" *The Spinners*

"Going in Circles" *The Friends of Distinction*

"Free" *Deniece Williams*

"Don't Mess With My Man" *Lucy Pearl*

"Happy" *Surface*

"After the Dance" *Fourplay featuring El DeBarge*

"You, Me and He" *Mtume*

"Neither One of Us" *Gladys Knight and the Pips*

"Home" *Stephanie Mills*

"I'm Going Down" *Rose Royce*

"You Can't See for Lookin'" *Betty Wright*

"After the Pain" *Betty Wright*

"Booga Bear" *Bobby Rush*

1
"Rain"

LaVonda

It smelled like rain the day I lost my mind.

As a matter of fact, the scent of rain clung to the air like an unfulfilled promise until the sun set. I spent that day, the entire day, sitting on my front porch, staring at nothing in particular. I can't say I was deep in thought because I wasn't. As a matter of fact, all that seemed to fill my head was static—white noise. It was as if someone had flipped the switch in my head from on to off.

I just sat there and rubbed my hand over my freshly-cut hair, the hair I'd had cut because I just didn't have the desire to keep it up, to go the beauty shop every week like I had in the past. I didn't eat or drink anything. I didn't use the toilet. I didn't answer the phone when it rang. I didn't smile or return the mailman's hello. I didn't wave when my neighbor greeted me. I didn't utter a word or move a muscle until the sun began its daily descent. And once the moon took its place in the sky, I stood from my seat, walked out into my yard and fell to the ground. Pressing my face into the grass, I cried for the rain, begged for it to stop playing around and go ahead and pour down on me. In my mind, the rain would make things better, maybe water down some of the pain. I writhed on the ground, pulling up handfuls of grass until my tears dried and transformed into soft wails.

"LaVonda? You all right?" my neighbor, Bunny, shrieked when she stepped outside her house and saw me. What a dumb question that was. I was rolling around on the ground begging for rain, wasn't I? Of course I wasn't okay. And then I saw the worried expression on her face and the ugly dress on her body and all I could do was laugh. I laughed so hard that I started to cry again. Then I got on my knees and began to crawl around the yard.

"I'ma go call your sister. Be right back," Bunny said.

I kept crawling and crying until I eventually crawled and cried the length of the yard and back. I really don't know how much time passed before my sister arrived. I do remember trying to swat her away from me. And I remember her yelling at someone. And I remember that I stopped crawling but I couldn't stop crying. The next and last thing I remember about that day is being shoved into an ambulance.

2
"Dark Times"

I sat on the passenger side of the car and watched as the world passed me by. Three weeks in the psych ward had done little to lift my mood, but my sister, Evetta, didn't know it. Neither did my doctor. I'd played the game, participated in group therapy. Taken the pills they gave me. Smiled when it was appropriate. Cried when they expected me to. And now I was free of that place and determined never to go back. But I was still depressed, not quite as insane as before, but definitely depressed. The depressive psychosis I was diagnosed with was gone, but Sister Blues was still an unwanted constant companion.

"I don't know why you don't just come and stay with me," she said, breaking into my foggy thoughts.

I turned and looked at her, gave her a weak smile. "I appreciate everything you've done for me, sis. Mama would be proud."

She sighed. "This is not about Mama, Von. I just want you to feel better."

For that to happen, you'd have to erase the past year, I thought. *Scratch that, you'd have to erase most of my life. And you know this is about you and Mama and not me.* "I feel fine, Evetta. Much better. Just need to get in my own tub and soak, and cook a meal in my own kitchen."

"Are you sure?"

"Yes. The memories just got to me. That's all."

"Won't the memories still be there, Von?"

I flinched a little. "I know how to cope with them now. The doctor taught me."

"Hmmm. Okay… I guess."

When we arrived at my home, I walked inside, ignoring Bunny's loud greeting. Evetta said something to her, probably apologized for my rudeness. I was sure she told her I was still out of it or high on meds or something like that. And the truth is, I didn't care. I never liked Bunny Smith or her terrible wardrobe or her henpecked husband. She could've kicked rocks for all I cared.

I walked through my spotless, silent house to my bedroom and sat at the foot of the bed I'd been unable to sleep in for months. The noiselessness might have been peaceful if I hadn't been aware that it wasn't always that way. I closed my eyes and tried to conjure up the sounds of the past but was met with nothing but more silence. The silence made it too easy to think. I was tired of thinking and rehashing and remembering… and regretting.

When I heard Evetta's voice echo through the house, I quickly ducked into the master bathroom and locked myself inside. Then I sat on the toilet and held my head in my hands.

"Von?" I heard her call through the door. "Von, are you already in the tub?"

"No, about to climb in, though."

"Oh… well, you want me to fix you some dinner? I need to get back home, but I can whip you something up real quick."

"No, you go ahead on home. I'll fix something."

"Well, if you're sure…"

"I am. Thanks, Evetta, love you."

"Love you, too, Von. I'll call you later. Don't forget to take your medicine." She was being so nice, but then again, I was in no condition to overtly defy her.

"All right. Tell Dan I said hey," I said as I gently placed the full bottle of antidepressants in the bottom of the trash can. While the depression cloaked me heavily in sadness, the pills numbed me completely. I wasn't sure which was worse.

"I sure will. Hey, Von?"

I sighed. "Yeah, Evetta?"

"I was thinking, maybe you could go back to school and finish that accounting degree. You were always so good with numbers and maybe school will take your mind off of things."

"Hmm, well, that's something to think about."

"Well, you be sure to think on it good. And Von?"

"Yes, Evetta?"

"Call me if you need me."

"I'll be fine, Evetta. I really will."

"Okay… bye."

"Bye."

I didn't sleep well that night. Disturbing images from my past haunted my dreams and I awakened to find my own tears soaking my pillow. A cloud of depression hung over me as I climbed out of bed and fixed myself a bowl of cereal that morning. It followed me into the shower and into the living room where I found it impossible to concentrate on a book I'd been wanting to read. The TV couldn't hold my attention, either. Nevertheless, I managed to fake my way through a phone conversation with Evetta. I assured her there was no need for her to come and check on me. And when I climbed into bed that night, my only prayer was that I'd be able to get some sleep.

3
"Zoom"

For the next week, there was more of the same. Minimal sleep at night, milling aimlessly around the house in the daytime, and pretending not to be depressed whenever my sister called. I used to love sitting on my porch and watching the world go by, but since my breakdown, that had become an acting exercise, too. I was afraid that if I just sat and stared, my neighbors would think I was losing it again and call my sister, and the daily phone calls from her were bad enough. I wouldn't be able to stand her coming to my house, hovering over me, threatening in her own sweet way to make full use of the power of attorney she'd secured during my hospitalization and have me readmitted. I knew she was itching to do it, to show me just how much control she could have over my life again. Like she did when we were kids. She'd molded me in her image as best she could for years, but that was before Wade.

As soon as his name entered my mind, I felt a squeezing in my chest and a quickening of my pulse. I hated thinking about him, remembering him. We were over in a final, no turning back, kind of way. I wished I could get over him, stop grieving for our relationship and feeling lonely, but things are never quite that easy when it comes to matters of the heart.

As I sat in my living room that spring afternoon, a week after being freed from the county hospital psych ward, the emptiness I'd been feeling inside for most of my life grew from a small, hollow place to a deep, bottomless crater in his absence. I wasn't used to being alone, and I missed Wade, there was no sense in trying to deny that. I hated myself for it. I hated myself for not being rational enough and strong enough to just let go. Why couldn't I just let go? I should've been happy to let go.

I wished I could go somewhere, to the movies, shopping, something, but I couldn't. Every time I ventured out, I could feel people's eyes on me, hear their whispers about poor, pitiful me. I just couldn't bear that. So I stayed at home.

I glanced around the room at the remnants of our life together, at the little knick-knacks and memories that still connected me to him, and realized I would never get better if I didn't get away from that house, that little narrow-minded town. If I didn't get away from that life that was, for all intents and purposes, over, I would never be able to move on or let go... *ever*. Then my mind shifted to Evetta, my dear, overbearing sister, Evetta. What would she say or think of me getting away for a bit? I mean, I had the money, plenty of it in the bank, so that wouldn't be an issue. But would she be okay with me being out of her reach?

You're an adult. This is your life. If you want to leave, then leave. Evetta is not your keeper.

The inner voice that spoke those words was not only crystal clear, but made more sense than my own voice had in a long time. All those years of being bossed around by the people I loved had muddled my thinking, made me mistrust my own instincts and thoughts, but it was true. I was an adult—forty-five years old. And sitting in that big house alone wasn't doing anything for my sanity. Even Evetta must've known that. After all, she'd suggested I stay with her. But there was no way on Earth I'd reside under her roof, under her rule and thumb, and with her husband. Especially not with her husband.

So with my mind made up, and the confidence that Evetta couldn't stop me even if she wanted to (and she'd definitely want to), not to mention the fact that there was no law that required me to tell anyone about my plans, I packed a couple of bags and loaded my car while it was still in the garage. Around midnight, when I was sure my neighbors, especially Bunny, were asleep, I locked up my house and left with no particular destination in mind.

4
"Cruisin'"

I'm not sure how long I drove, but I do remember the night eventually dawning into day. By 5:00 AM, my eyelids had become so heavy I knew it was no longer safe for me to be operating my vehicle. I knew I was somewhere on the southern edge of Arkansas, poised to exit my home state, but it was another ten minutes before a sign informed me that I was entering a town, Hyacinth Valley— population 1053.

I smiled as I passed the sign and wondered to myself how the census takers had managed to count the citizens with such accuracy. I also wondered if this little town had at least one motel to boast about. I hoped so, because I was absolutely exhausted and since I'd been suffering from insomnia, I looked forward to getting some sleep.

I pulled over at a gas station and went inside to see if there was any lodging nearby. The lot and adjacent store were empty, save the neatly stocked shelves and the rather unenthusiastic clerk. "Excuse me," I said, giving the short, painfully thin, even brown-skinned woman a warm smile.

She lazily looked up from her magazine and locked eyes with me, but didn't say a word.

I softly cleared my throat and said, "Um, is there a motel or hotel around here?"

She sighed as she closed her copy of *Essence Magazine* and said,

"Yeah, there's a bed and breakfast up the road a bit. You can see if they'll take you."

See if they'll take me? Was this a "whites only" bed and breakfast or something? "Oh, okay. Thanks."

"It's called Hyacinth Manor. Big yellow house, used to be a plantation," she added. "Can't miss the sign on the side of the road."

A plantation?

Oh, Lord, I thought. For a second, I wondered if I should just keep driving until I reached the next town. Then I yawned and knew it was best to try my luck at the plantation-cum-bed and breakfast.

Luckily, the clerk was correct. It only took me five minutes to reach a white wooden sign sitting beside a driveway that informed me I'd arrived at the Hyacinth Manor. And below the name, in bold black letters, it read: "Lodging by invitation only." I now understood what the lady had meant when she said, "…if they'll take you." I'd never heard of a bed and breakfast you had to be invited to before. Turning onto the long, wide driveway and coasting though the majestic alley of oaks, I could see the house in the distance and it was absolutely gorgeous; magnificent-looking in an inviting shade of yellow.

I pulled my car to a stop in front of the colossal house and sighed as I stepped onto the driveway and made my way up the steps to the front door, silently praying they would at least give me a room for a few hours so I could sleep off my exhaustion. As I entered the beautifully decorated foyer and walked to the front desk, I felt my hands begin to shake with anxiety. I stopped in my tracks, took a deep breath, and approached the desk again. A striking older woman with a gorgeous salt and pepper afro and a bright smile greeted me. "Good morning and welcome to Hyacinth Manor. May I help you?"

I returned her smile with a road-weary one of my own. "Yes, I see that you all are an invitation-only establishment but I've been on the road for hours and I really just need to sleep for a little while; I just need a bit of rest but I'm willing to pay the regular rate."

She lifted a perfectly-trimmed eyebrow and stared at me for a moment, and then she said in a gentle voice, "Are you sure you don't need a room for longer? Looks to me like you need more than just a little bit of rest."

Taken aback, I replied, "I... I don't know. I just..."

She smiled again. "My name is Rosa, I am the proprietor of this place, and I'm extending an invitation for you to stay here for as long as you need, sugar."

I frowned slightly. "Oh... okay. Thank you."

"You're welcome. Just a moment. Rochelle!"

Seconds later, a very curvaceous and very pretty younger woman wearing an interesting-looking, tribal-patterned jumpsuit and waist-length box braids arrived. "Yes, Ms. Rosa?"

"This is—I'm sorry, sugar, I didn't get your name," Rosa said, her attention on me again.

"LaVonda Ingram," I replied. "Do you need my credit card?"

"We'll take care of that later, sugar. Rochelle, take Miss LaVonda here to Room Ten."

"Room Ten?" Rochelle repeated with wide eyes.

"Yes, *Room Ten*."

"Okay… um, follow me," Rochelle said.

As I trailed her up the wide staircase, I asked, "Is Room Ten haunted or something?"

She chuckled. "Oh, no. As a matter of fact, it's the best room in the house. Not many people are allowed in there."

"Oh," I said.

Once in the room, she rattled off the times of meals which she said could only be eaten in the dining room, showed me where the remote controls and channel guides were for the TV, and informed me that there were fresh towels and soap in the adjoining bathroom. She'd barely left and closed the door behind her when I fell into the bed and into a deep sleep.

5
"On My Own"

When I finally woke up, the room was dark and a quick peek out of
the window told me that night had fallen. I groggily stood from the
bed and took in the dark surroundings I had ignored when I first
arrived due to exhaustion. I switched on the bedside lamp and the
room came to life in the soft lighting. It was huge, complete with a
king-sized canopy bed that I could now confirm was very
comfortable, a sitting area with a fireplace, and a private bathroom.
It was decorated mostly in hunter green. Gorgeous green-on-green,
pinstriped wallpaper covered the walls, and a beautiful vase of lime-
green hydrangeas adorned the dresser. The dark mahogany furniture,
along with the décor, gave it a cozy, homey feel. It was an absolutely
lovely room, a room I could see myself spending many days in.

I took a seat on the sofa in the sitting area and soaked up the
tranquility that emanated from the walls. Something about being
here, away from my home and everyone I knew and wished I could
forget, eased my troubled soul. I had switched my phone off before
leaving and I felt a lightness in being free from my sister's
smothering ways. I did realize, however, that I'd have to call her
eventually, just so she wouldn't think something horrible had
happened to me since I was in a "fragile" state of mind.

My eyes shifted to a painting hanging over the fireplace. It was of
a woman, a breathtaking Rubenesque woman with deep chocolate
skin and enviable curves. She was lounging on a bed and she was

naked. Her breasts were concealed by the cascades of wavy black hair that hung lazily from her head. A thin white sheet was draped strategically across her lap, covering her womanhood. Her eyes were closed and there was a faint smile on her face. It was, hands down, the most beautiful piece of art I'd ever laid eyes on. Anyone who looked at it could feel that it was a labor of love. The artist had not only known his subject, he had known her *intimately*.

I wondered who the artist was since I couldn't make out the scribbled signature in the lower right-hand corner of the painting. I also wondered if the owner was willing to sell it. It truly spoke to me.

I moved closer to it, tried to stretch my 5'5" body taller to better see the signature in the corner, but from my vantage point, the sloppily scrawled moniker looked like hieroglyphics.

I sighed, felt my stomach rumble, and tried to remember what the lady had told me about dinner. Then I remembered I still needed to give them my credit card information. I walked into the green bathroom, freshened up, and then left the comfortable confines of Room Ten. Downstairs, I found the lobby empty and the front desk unmanned. I smelled food and decided to follow the aroma in hopes of satisfying my hunger, hoping that I wasn't too late. If there was just a taste of something left, I was sure I could make it until breakfast the next day and maybe hit the road by late morning and head to—I had no idea where I was going.

There were no people in the huge dining room, which was bathed in shades of warm brown and cream, but a long table against the south wall still held trays of food kept warm by small burners. I quickly crossed the room, grabbed a plate, and began piling mixed salad, roasted potatoes, and big juicy roasted chicken breasts onto it, along with a healthy portion of green beans and a gigantic yeast roll. I sat in one of the insanely comfortable chairs at the table, which looked to seat at least twelve people, and had finished half of my meal before realizing I hadn't fixed myself anything to drink. As if on cue, a small, mature, bronze-skinned woman entered the dining room from what I assumed was the kitchen. She wore a white apron that swallowed her petite frame, and a hairnet that covered her fluffy red hair. I could see the youthful sparkle in her eyes behind her rectangular glasses as she smiled at me and said, "Oh, hi. Didn't know anyone was still in here. I'm Ms. Dorcas. So you're the lady in Room Ten?

I returned her smile, nodded. "Yes, LaVonda Ingram."

"Nice to meet you." She frowned as her eyes fell on my plate. "You want some sweet tea?"

"Yes, ma'am."

She nodded, ducked back into the kitchen, and returned with a tall glass of tea. Then she just stood there and smiled at me. Feeling a little awkward, I said, "The food is wonderful. Did you cook it?"

"Mm-hmm, I cook all the food around here."

I smiled again.

"Well, enjoy. And I already know you'll enjoy Room Ten," she said before disappearing into the kitchen again. She popped her head out the door and added, "Just leave your dishes on the table when you're done."

"Okay."

I finished my food, made my way back to my room, and easily fell into a dreamless slumber.

6
"Papillion"

The distant buzzing of a lawn mower awakened me the next morning. My heart raced as I fought the covers and stumbled out of bed to the window. I pulled the heavy drapes back, expecting to see Wade making neat lines in our front yard, having forgotten where and when I was. Instead, my eyes were graced by a tall shirtless man who was definitely *not* Wade. This man was built, with muscles that shone with sweat. The smooth brown skin of his back glistened in the early May sun. When he turned around, I couldn't make out his facial features but saw that he sported a full beard; his head was covered with a black scarf. I never liked the rugged type, but there was something about this man that held my attention. Probably the muscles.

I stood there and watched him for a few more minutes, wishing I could get a better look at his face, and then I wondered why I wanted to get a better look at his face. The mere fact that he was cutting the yard of a former plantation was a turn-off for me, or it should've been. Wade was a white collar worker, made plenty of money, and I had the car, house, and lifestyle to prove it.

But what good is that doing you now?

I shook my head and sighed as the image of the man who'd been my life partner flashed before me. An image of him in a white tuxedo, reaching toward me to lead me in a dance—our wedding reception. I missed that man whether I wanted to miss him or not.

Thankfully, my hollow stomach pulled me from the past back into the present and I shuffled into the bathroom and went about the business of making myself presentable.

After another failed attempt to pay for my room, as the front desk was unmanned again that morning, I went to the dining room to find it empty except for the delicious-smelling food. I made my plate and was digging into half of a grapefruit when the unmistakable scents of grass and gasoline hit my nose. My first thought was that it was the lawn mower guy, my second thought was how rude it was of him to come into the guest dining area reeking of grass and gas, and my third thought—well, I'm not sure what my third thought was because I happened to look up and into the nicest pair of dark eyes I'd ever seen. Then my eyes scanned the rest of his face—strong nose, Darnell Williams-caliber thick lips that parted into a handsome smile, smooth coffee-with-no-creamer-colored skin. And when he said "Hi", his voice was as rich as a thick slice of New York cheesecake. I mumbled hi in response and began to nervously mutilate my grapefruit with my spoon. He gave me a little nod as he slid his work gloves off his hands and shoved them into the back pockets of his jeans. Thankfully, he now had on a black V-neck t-shirt. Had he still been shirtless, I might have started drooling.

He walked over to the kitchen door, knocked, and glanced back at me. I dropped my eyes and tried to remember my own name.

The kitchen door swung open and Ms. Dorcas reached up and hugged the sweaty Adonis. "Have a seat. I'll get your plate," she said.

"Yes, ma'am," he replied and then took a seat—directly across from me. My hand trembled so badly that I gave up trying to take a sip of water.

"I'm August," he said.

I looked up at his face. Lord, his face, his face, *his face!* "I'm..." I still hadn't figured out my name.

He raised his eyebrows, his eyes glued to me.

"Von," I finally said. "My name is Von."

"Nice to meet you. I hope you're enjoying your stay."

I nodded. "I am." *And I'm enjoying the view, too,* I thought.

Ms. Dorcas emerged from the kitchen with a foil-covered plate. She handed it to August and said, "I see you've met our guest."

He stood from the table and leaned over and kissed her cheek. "Yes, ma'am. Thank you, again, Ms. Dorcas."

"Sure thing, baby."

I watched him leave and felt the numbness leave my brain. I took an unsteady sip of my water and then remembered Ms. Dorcas was still in the room with me. She was grinning from ear to ear as she said, "Fine, ain't he?" Then she turned and entered the kitchen with a chuckle.

Hell, yeah, I thought.

***

Who the hell was this August guy and why couldn't I stop thinking about him and why was he so doggone handsome and fine?

Why did he make my ovaries quiver? Had I finished losing my mind?

As I stood in my room, staring out the window at the neatly cut backyard of the massive house, I had to wonder what I was hoping to see. Then I answered my own question—August. August, August, August. But why would I think I stood a chance of seeing him again? I was sure he was done cutting the grass. He was probably long gone, back to his home and the lucky woman who shared his bed. Wait, what if he was gay? And why did I care? I should've been on the road to somewhere, nowhere, by now. But August.

August.

I didn't even know his last name, his age, *nothing*.

I closed my eyes and slumped onto the sofa. I released a frustrated sigh and then heard a sound that made me bolt to my feet. A weed eater. A weed eater!

I rushed to the window, hoping it was him. Hoping he wasn't a part of some grass crew. Hoping it wasn't some other person manning the piece of equipment. But he was nowhere in sight. No one was, yet the loud whirring of the weed eater continued. I stood there for a ridiculously long time, so long that I finally had to remind myself I was too old and too married for this; at least, technically I was still married.

The whirring continued and I prayed for my curiosity to leave. I hoped this insane infatuation would flee. I didn't want to obsess over this man as a replacement for my obsessive depression. I couldn't help but think maybe I should've brought my pills with me, probably shouldn't have thrown them away.

Then my mind shifted to Evetta. I knew she must've been frantic. So I took a deep breath, released it, and dug my cell phone out of the hip pocket of my blue jeans. I turned it on, dialed her number, and held my breath as it rang in my ear.

"Von! I've been worried sick! Where are you?" she screamed into my ear once the call connected.

"Hey, Evetta. Just wanted to let you know I'm good. Just needed to get away for a bit," I said calmly.

"Away? Away where?"

"Hmm, I'm not really sure," I semi-lied. "Somewhere in Arkansas."

"What do you mean, *somewhere in Arkansas? I'm* somewhere in Arkansas. Did someone make you leave with them?"

"No, I drove myself. I'm just taking some time for myself. Being in that house was just... I needed to be somewhere else."

"You could've come and stayed with us. I even offered."

"No, I'm fine here."

"Where is here, Von?"

"I'll let you go. I'll call you in a few days. Love you."

"Wait, Von. Tell me where you—"

I ended the call, shut my phone back off, and stared out the window again. My mind drifted back to my childhood, to all the nights my mother worked the graveyard shift at a local factory. All those nights Evetta would cook and clean, help me with my homework, and put me to bed. From the time she was ten and I was five, Evetta was my caregiver and more of a mother to me than my real mother, Pauline, ever was. When our mother dropped dead at work when I was only fourteen, a nineteen-year-old Evetta took me into the house she shared with the boyfriend who would become her husband and raised me. She had promised our mother, who always had a fear of dying, that she would look out for me, and she had fulfilled that promise in a devoted, fanatically smothering way. It was nearly impossible for me to breathe around Evetta. I had no clarity when I was around her. Her presence was stifling. I knew she loved me and I loved her, too. I just wished more than anything that she could learn to be my sister instead of my overseer.

With a heavy heart and full mind, I climbed into bed and let the continuous whirring of the weed eater lull me to sleep.

***

I tucked my credit card in my bra as I passed the ever-empty front desk on my way to dinner, since I'd slept through lunch. I was surprised to see not only Ms. Rosa and Rochelle already seated at the table, eating... but August, too. And he was no longer sweaty. The odors of grass and gasoline were not apparent and he was wearing clean jeans and a red t-shirt. His wild, thick, coarse hair was exposed. He smiled when I entered the room. I smiled back, my eyes glued to him as I took a seat at the table. After exchanging greetings with everyone, the butterflies in my stomach became rather aggressive and I realized they had more to do with hunger than

August's presence. I also realized I was the only person at the table without a plate, and reminded myself that there was a buffet table in the room. So I stood on shaky legs and prayed my hands would be steady enough for me to make a plate. The whole time I inched my way down the buffet line, his name screamed in my head over and over again like an overexcited cheerleader with a megaphone—August! August! Auuuuuugust!

I was alone in a strange place, and still mending a broken heart. Yes, all of that would explain my visceral reaction to him.

Tall, handsome *him*.

I reclaimed my seat at the table, closed my eyes and said grace, and opened them to see that everyone had left except for August. My insides liquefied instantly. My hunger dissipated. I had to fight not to stare at him.

"Where are you from?" he asked. Was he talking to me? Of course he was. I was the only other person there.

"Um... here, I mean, here in Arkansas," I stammered. "You?"

"Here, mostly—Hyacinth Valley. Well, I grew up here. Was born in Ohio, lived all over before coming back here."

If his voice hadn't wrapped itself around my heart and squeezed, I might have asked him about his travels, dug deeper into his past, but instead I said, "That's nice."

Silence fell between us as we both dug into our meals. I glanced up at him often to find his eyes on his plate. He was stunning, the most beautiful man I'd ever seen. As badly as I wanted to pretend I wasn't attracted to him, my body wouldn't let me.

"How long will you be staying?" he asked.

"I'm not sure yet."

He nodded and gave me an understanding look, as if my indecision made perfect sense to him.

More silence, bar the clanking of silverware against plates and the thud of glasses against the table.

He finished before I did and stood from the table, smiled at me, and said, "Well, I'll see you later. Have a good rest of the evening."

I returned his smile. "Same to you."

7
"In the Morning"

I dreamt of August and his voice that night. And when I awakened the next morning, I was eager to get to breakfast in hopes of him being at the table when I got there. This time I didn't bother taking my credit card with me, figuring if Ms. Rosa wasn't worried about it, why should I be? I showered, dressed, and lathered my body in my favorite Bath and Body Works lotion. I even slid a little lip gloss on my lips, and made sure my closely-cropped natural was brushed. I felt like I was back in high school, when I had a crush on a light-skinned, hazel–eyed boy named Duncan White. Man did I have it bad for him, and it seemed I had it just as bad for August Last-Name-Unknown.

Upon arriving in the dining room, I was disappointed to find it empty, but held onto the hope that he would at least come for a to-go plate.

Maybe.

Prayerfully.

I was nearly done with my meal when Ms. Rosa joined me, wearing a flowing caftan and matching turban. I surmised that she must've lived in Hyacinth Manor and wondered why I hadn't bothered to learn more about the place and its inhabitants. I also wondered if I was the only guest, and what was up with the "invitation only" thing? Absent of August's brand of magic, my mind was clear enough to be curious about other things.

"Good morning, sugar," Ms. Rosa said cheerily as she floated toward the buffet line.

"Good morning."

"Forgive me for not asking you this earlier, but are you enjoying your stay?" she asked, her back to me as she fixed her plate.

"Oh, yes. Everything is wonderful."

"Satisfied with your room?"

"Yes, very."

She took a seat across from me as I played with what was left of my meal, my eyes darting toward the door nearly every second.

"He doesn't eat in here that often," Ms. Rosa said.

"Ma'am?"

"August. He rarely eats in here. Lives in one of the former slave houses on the property, though, back in the woods."

"Oh…" Was I that obvious?

"He keeps this place looking nice, makes any necessary repairs."

"I… I see."

"He's about forty, I think, never been married. No children. A very, very nice young man, kind-hearted. He's like a son to me. Me and his mama were childhood friends. God rest her soul."

I stared at the gray-haired woman for a moment. "Ms. Rosa, I didn't—"

Her eyes met mine and a warm smile spread across her face. "You didn't have to, sugar."

My face began to heat up.

"You like taking walks?"

"Walks? Uh, yes, I suppose." I really wasn't sure what I liked at that point, was used to others deciding so many things for me—Wade, Evetta.

"There is a set of patio doors in the sitting room that lead out back, and there's a path that cuts through the woods behind the manor. Makes for a lovely, peaceful walk. You look like you could use one." And with that, she picked up her plate of half-eaten food. "I think I'll finish this in my room. You feel free to roam and explore all you'd like, sugar."

***

After breakfast, I returned to my room when what I really wanted to do was find out where the old slave quarters were and get a glimpse of August. Okay, what I actually wanted to do was strip naked and climb his tall, strong body and ravish him. One thing I could thank August for was the fact that I was too infatuated with him to be depressed. He was a natural antidepressant wrapped in smooth brown flesh and defined muscles.

I sat in my room for a full hour, fighting my own desire to look for him. At one point, I switched on my phone with the intent of calling Evetta, but when text message after text message popped up—fifty-four in total and all from her—saying things like "where are you" and "please call me", I quickly turned my phone back off, left my room, found the peach and cream color-themed sitting room, exited through the patio doors, and slowly trekked across the huge backyard and onto the trail that led into the woods.

It *was* a peaceful walk, and I did feel myself relax as I wandered among the towering trees and listened to the rustling of leaves as small squirrels scurried about and birds fluttered from tree to tree. I became lost in thoughts of my life back home, my childhood, and my marriage. Thoughts of the handsome, copper-skinned Wade Ingram inundated my mind, and so lost was I in those thoughts that I lost awareness of my surroundings. So when I heard his voice, I was startled into paralysis.

"Hi, there," he said.

I stood still, my heart pounding fiercely as if attempting to escape my chest. I turned and saw him sitting on the ground, his back against a tree as he twirled a stick around in his hand. Somehow, with sweat shimmering on his brow, he looked even more handsome.

"Nice day for a walk," he continued.

I nodded, still glued to that spot on the path. "Yes, it is," I managed to say.

He sat there with a smile on his face, his eyes fixed on mine. In return, I stared at him, letting my eyes follow him as he got to his feet and slowly walked toward me. My breath caught in my throat when he stopped right in front of me, tilted his head, and kissed me. Almost reflexively, I closed my eyes and relaxed as he pulled me to him and let his hands rest on my hips.

As he deepened the kiss, I wrapped my arms around his sweaty body and pressed mine against it. When we parted, I ached to feel the warmth of his body again. Instead, he just stood there and stared at me and I stared back. Minutes passed before he turned and began walking further down the path, and I robotically followed him. I felt like I was having an out-of-body experience. I had no idea who this man really was, where he was going, or why I was following him. I just knew I had to, *needed* to. Then I suppose a little common sense kicked in and I stopped dead in my tracks. I watched as he progressed down the path. Then I turned and ran back to the house.

8
"Amorous"

Back in my room, I tried to sort things out, wondered why he'd kissed me, why I'd kissed him back, why it felt so... *good*, better than anything I'd ever felt before, and why I desperately wanted more of it. I would've given myself to him. I was sure of that. Had I followed him to wherever he was going, no matter where that was, I would've gladly given myself to him over and over again.

How could he have an effect on me that the man I'd spent most of my life with had never had? Why could I still feel him and smell him? Why did I miss him like I'd known him all my life?

When a knock came at the door, my heart skipped six or seven beats. Was it him? If so, would I be able to control myself around him?

"Yes?" I called through the door, unsure if I could trust my tired, wobbly legs enough to walk.

"It's Rochelle."

I stumbled to my feet and to the door, opened it, and offered her a weak smile as I was still under the effects of August.

"Ms. Rosa wanted me to invite you to tea."

"Oh, when is it?"

"In ten minutes. In the sitting room."

"Okay, thank you."

Rochelle nodded slightly and then left.

I closed the door, having already decided I wouldn't be taking her up on the offer, and then I thought that maybe they could fill me in on August and decided to hit the bathroom before joining them for tea.

***

"First, let's welcome LaVonda," Rosa said.

"Welcome," the other three ladies said. I smiled and thanked Rochelle, Ms. Dorcas, and a tall, husky but shapely young lady named Dee Dee, who had been the one to clean my room every day since my arrival.

"LaVonda, we always have tea once a week but it's usually just us staff. I figured since you're our only guest, it'd be nice for you to join us."

"Well, thank you for inviting me," I said as I added sugar to my piping hot cup of tea. I was sitting on a very comfortable loveseat. Rosa and Ms. Dorcas occupied the sofa. Rochelle and Dee Dee rounded out the circle of women in dining room chairs.

"Well, what we do is vent about whatever non-work-related thing that's bothering us—kids, men, whatever. We all take turns sharing and you are welcome to join in."

I took a sip of tea and said, "Uh—okay."

"Well, I want to go first," Rochelle said, setting her cup on the coffee table. "Justin."

"Oh, Lord," the other women chorused.

"What is that boy up to now?" Rosa said then looked at me.

"Justin is Rochelle's son."

"My *only* child," Rochelle added, "and I swear that boy is gonna be the death of me. Now he's flunking English. I just don't understand it. He's such a smart boy. I'm almost fifty, I'm too old for this."

If Rochelle was almost fifty, she sure wore it well. *Man, black really doesn't crack*, I thought.

"How's his Spanish? Didn't you say his daddy is Puerto Rican?" Dee Dee asked. "Maybe English is just not his thing."

"His daddy is *half* Puerto Rican and since his only contribution has come in the form of child support checks, he's had no influence on Justin's language skills. And in all the time I was with him, I never heard him speak Spanish. I don't think he knows how. Anyway, sometimes I just wish I had someone to help me with Justin. My parents help all that they can, but his father's input would mean so much right about now. But that's a lost cause. That boy will be a man soon. I feel like I'm running out of time with him."

"Hmm, I know the feeling. You know I raised Man by myself. Dorcas, you know how it is, right?"

"Shoot, yeah. I had a husband but he was from the old school. Never lifted a finger to help me raise those kids except to whoop 'em, may he rest in peace."

"Y'all gonna make me never have kids," Dee Dee said. "What about you, LaVonda? You got any kids?"

My eyes widened. "Um... no, no kids."

"Well, I got man problems," Ms. Dorcas said.

"Oooh, Ms. Dorcas!" Rochelle exclaimed.

"Aww, hush, girl. I'm old, not dead."

"Now, Dorcas Malone, who are you messing around with?" Rosa asked.

"Humph, I ain't messing around with nobody, but Farris Kenwood *wants* to mess around."

"Farris Kenwood?!" The other three women shrieked in unison. I must've looked as clueless as I felt because Rochelle turned to me and said, "He's known to be an old player, a *rich* one."

"Well, rich or not, I told him ain't no one playing on my merry-go-round without buying a ticket to the whole amusement park. He gon' have to put a ring on it."

All of the women burst into laughter, including me.

Ms. Dorcas, who looked to be every bit of seventy years old, patted what I had come to realize was a red wig, and said, "I don't know what the hell y'all laughing at. I ain't no cheap thrill."

"How long y'all been seeing each other, Dorcas?" Rosa asked.

"A couple of months."

"And you're ready for marriage already?" Dee Dee chimed in.

"Old as we are? Heck yeah I'm ready!"

Snickers filled the room as the other women began to discuss their relationship woes. Dee Dee was tired of her long-time, live-in boyfriend's job hopping.

"Like my cousin Gwen Guthrie would say, ain't nothing going on but the rent, but that man of mine act like it's gonna pay itself!" she declared.

I frowned and looked at Rochelle who just shook her head. I had to bite my lip to keep from laughing.

The only man in Rochelle's life other than her son was his deadbeat father, a man she virtually despised, and she made it clear she never wanted to fall in love again because of him. Rosa was happy to report that she was still just as intentionally single as she'd always been.

"What about you, LaVonda? You married? Dating?" Ms. Dorcas asked.

No, but I'm obsessed with a guy named August. "No, I'm-uh, a... widow."

The women collectively offered their condolences and then the room fell silent. My sad life had dampened the mood.

"He died a year ago," I heard myself say. "Been having a hard time dealing with it. Can't seem to let go..." I couldn't believe I'd said that.

"Mmm, I knew you were here for a reason. This place has healing powers. You're right where you need to be," Rosa said with the other ladies nodding in unison.

"Mm-hmm, especially in Room Ten," Dee Dee added. The other women agreed.

"What's so special about that room?" I asked.

"I think I got the dishwasher fixed for you, Ms. Dorcas."

My tea cup rattled on its saucer at the sound of his voice. I didn't dare look up at him as I set the cup down and forced myself not to rush to him and wrap my legs around his waist.

"Thank you, August. Want some tea?" Ms. Dorcas asked.

"Yes, ma'am, I'd love some," he replied, and then he did something that made my entire body stand at attention; he sat *right next to me* on the loveseat. From that point on all I could do was sit there and remind myself to breathe as my body temperature began to slowly rise. I shoved my unsteady hands under my thighs and fixed my eyes on the floral-patterned rug beneath my feet. I could smell his sweat, a scent that was beginning to become both familiar and appealing to me, and though I kept my eyes away from him, the image of his face dominated my thoughts.

I glanced around the now painfully quiet room to see all eyes on me—including August's—and I reacted in the only way I knew how. I stood from my seat and softly said, "Um, excuse me." And before anyone could reply, I had swiftly left the room, made it to the stairs, and was heading back to Room Ten.

"Wait!" I heard him call.

But I couldn't stop my feet from ascending the stairs. As I fumbled with my door key, I felt him rest his hand on my shoulder. "Von, wait. Why do you keep running away from me? Is it this?" He spun me around and kissed me again... and I let him. As a matter of fact, I felt relieved, like this was what I'd been needing for a long time. Maybe it was.

His lips left mine and I instantly missed them. "Yes," I whispered, my eyes downcast.

He lifted my chin, held my eyes with his. "You didn't like it?"

"I did. That's the problem."

"Well, what about this?" He leaned in and gently suckled my neck.

I shuddered, grabbed his head, and held it in place. Then a wave of shame hit me and I pulled away from him. "I don't know what I'm doing."

"You're enjoying me," he whispered as he pinned me to the door and went to work on the other side of my neck. "And I'm enjoying you..."

"I don't even know your last name," I said breathily.

"Donovan. August Donovan."

"I don't know you."

He lifted his head and gently kissed my lips again. "Meet me on the path after breakfast tomorrow."

I looked into his chocolate eyes and almost involuntarily said, "Okay."

9
"A Long Walk"

I barely slept that night, my mind reeling with thoughts of August Donovan, my skin vibrating with the memory of his touch and his kisses, my soul longing for his presence. I had never wanted time to pass so badly before in my life. The way I felt about August, the madness I experienced just from being around him, made me question my relationship with my late husband. Sure, I had loved him and he had been a good provider, but this, whatever this was that I felt for August, was totally different. It was uninhibited and free. Just the thought of him made me feel unsteady, unsure, afraid, and totally exhilarated, all at the same time. And for someone who had been overseen or controlled in some way by other people for nearly all of her life, I liked the free-falling sensation Mr. August Donovan evoked.

When morning finally came, I rose from the bed with butterflies furiously fluttering in my stomach. I rushed through my shower, taking extra care with lotioning and perfuming my body, before pulling on a simple tank top and denim shorts that hugged my wide hips and thick thighs. Then I slipped on my sneakers, checked my make-up-free face in the mirror, and headed downstairs to breakfast.

I decided to eat light and only had fruit with my coffee. I was glad no one else was in the dining room, as I was too excited to hold anyone a decent conversation. Before I knew it, I was striding across the sprawling backyard toward the path. I walked for several minutes, the fluttering of my abdominal butterflies becoming even more frantic. Anxiety invaded me and I suddenly felt foolish for wandering around in the woods alone in anticipation of meeting a man I barely knew. What would Evetta think?

Screw Evetta, the inner voice said. I was poised to argue with it when I heard, "Good morning."

I spun around to find him standing against a tree, and a smile instantly spread across my semi-sweaty face. I wanted to step into his arms and never leave. More than that, I wanted to feel his lips on mine.

As if he'd read my mind, he moved closer to me with a smile on his own face and quickly claimed my mouth, pulling me so close to him that to the animals around us we must've appeared to be one person. We stood there in the middle of that path for what felt like forever and a single second at the same time. His kisses were too much for me but I wanted more.

When we parted, he reached for my hand and grasped it tightly as he led me further down the path, stopping every few steps to kiss my lips, my cheeks, my neck, my hands.

"What are we doing?" I asked as we strolled down the path.

He stopped in his tracks, smiled, and kissed my nose. "Courting."

I smiled, too. "How can you court someone you barely know?"

"By getting to know them." He kissed my lips. "Like this."

"Don't you think we should talk?"

He grasped my hand again. "We will."

When we reached a small, log cabin-like wooden structure, he stopped and said, "We're here."

"Where?"

"My home."

I followed him inside, remembering that Ms. Rosa said he lived in a former slave house, and felt my mood shift a little. I was still excited to be with him, but standing inside that edifice was slightly sobering.

"This is the only one left," he said. "The rest were either torn down or fell down over time. Years ago, these houses stood in a clearing but a former owner, a white man, let nature take its course so now you can no longer see this area from the big house because of the trees."

I let my eyes roam. This was the sitting or living room I supposed, but there was no sofa or chairs. It was clean, if nearly bare, with only a mattress and box springs adorned with messy white sheets occupying the middle of the room. There was also one of those huge old wooden stereo consoles in one corner. That was it.

"When Ms. Rosa acquired the place, she had this house fixed up, converted the one room into four small rooms—a living room, bathroom, bedroom, and kitchen. She had it wired up for electricity, had plumbing installed. But I don't think she ever meant for anyone to live here. When I got back in town and she agreed to hire me on, she gave me a room in the big house. One day I was out exploring the property and I found this place. When I asked her about it, she said she'd fixed it up to pay homage to our people. I begged her to let me live here. Been here ever since."

My eyes swept over the room again and then landed on him. "Why did you want to live here? It seems like such a sad place."

"Sad? No. Inspiring? Yes."

I frowned slightly. "How so?"

"Do you realize how strong our ancestors had to be? I mean, you and I are proof of that merely by existing and having brown skin at the same time. We're here because they were strong enough to survive, because they didn't give up. When I look around this place I see nothing but victory, triumph."

His enthusiasm was so contagious I couldn't help but smile a little. "You sleep in here?" I asked.

"Yes. I use the bedroom for storage," he said and then walked over to the stereo and opened the doors of the ancient-looking cabinet to reveal a modest album collection. In his jeans and blue t-shirt, he crouched down and thumbed through the records, chose one, lifted the top of the console, and placed the record on the turntable that was hidden inside. After a series of pops and crackles, the familiar intro to LTD's "We Both Deserve Each Other's Love" began to play.

"Dance with me, Von," he said.

Without hesitation, I stepped into his arms, rested my head on his broad chest, and closed my eyes as Jeffrey Osborne's soulful tenor voice serenaded us. I felt so at home in this stranger's arms it was downright weird, but it felt so good. "Who are you?" I asked as we swayed to the music, our feet sliding across the spotless wood floor.

"I'm August, a man who appreciates rare and beautiful things…

like you."

My cheeks began to flush. He stopped dancing, stepped back, and gazed at me. "I appreciate your beautiful eyes, your cute nose, your full lips—*especially* your full lips."

My old behind giggled lightly.

He ran a finger down the side of my neck. "And this skin, my favorite shade of brown."

"What shade is that?"

"Hmm, burnt sienna."

"Burnt sienna," I repeated.

As he pulled me back into his arms, he said, "Yeah."

We danced to an entire side of that album and then he changed the record to Marvin Gaye's "What's Going On," informing me that it was his favorite. He took a seat on his bed and beckoned for me to join him. At forty-five, I should've had enough sense to run up out of that cabin, away from the madness and danger this man presented. Yet, I didn't. I walked over to him and sat beside him. He held my hand and we just sat there and listened to Marvin share his heart and wisdom with us and before I even realized it, we'd both fallen asleep, me with my head resting on his shoulder.

***

"Who are *you*, Von?" he asked as we sat on his bed having a lunch of ham sandwiches and iced tea.

"Hmm, I'm someone who doesn't usually do things like this."

"Like what? Eat ham sandwiches?"

I chuckled. "No, be spontaneous. My life has always pretty much been mapped out for me. Never had to make many decisions for myself."

"Really?"

I nodded. "Yeah. My sister picked my clothes for me when we were girls, then she picked my college, even picked out the boyfriend who would eventually become my husband. After I got married, my husband made my decisions for me—picked out our house, our cars, our vacation spots, approved or vetoed my clothes. This, *us*—this is different for me." I was a little surprised at my own candor but it felt good to share a part of myself with him.

"Different good or different bad?"

I smiled. "Different *very* good."

He leaned in and kissed me. "Glad to know that."

"Where did you live before you came back here?"

He shrugged. "Just about everywhere. My work required me to travel a lot."

"What kind of work did you do?"

A strange look landed on his face and quickly disappeared. "Doesn't matter. What matters is that I came back here three years ago and it took all that time for God to send me my other half."

A warmth filled me from head to toe.

"What happened to your husband, Von?"

"He died."

"I'm sorry."

I sighed. "Me, too."

"You still love him?"

"Sometimes. But it's fading."

He nodded.

"Have you ever been married? How old are you?" I asked, wanting and needing to know all I could about him.

"Never been married and I'm forty-five. How old are you?"

"I'm forty-five, too."

He gasped. "I don't believe it! I thought you were twenty-five for sure."

"I bet you did."

"You run like a twenty-five-year-old."

I blushed and shrugged.

We talked until the sun began to set about everything from soul music to old black films to politics to history. August was smart and I loved listening to him. We talked through dinnertime into bedtime and I spent the night fully clothed and in his arms, waking up in the middle of the night and wondering if I should pinch myself.

"You feel that?" he asked, his voice piercing the early morning darkness.

"What?" I replied.

"Our hearts. They're beating as one."

I lay there for several minutes to find that sure enough, our hearts were beating in unison.

10
"Being with You"

I awakened the next morning to find myself alone in August's bed and wondered where he was. I only had to roll over to find him. He was kneeling on the floor, his face pressed against the wood, and I assumed he was praying. I watched until he lifted his head and effortlessly hopped to his feet.

"Are you a Muslim?" I asked, not that it really mattered to me.

"No, I'm a Christian, I just find the more humble the position, the more powerful the prayer."

I dropped my eyes. I was sort of a Christian but I couldn't remember the last time I prayed, not even after Wade died. Not even when I slipped into the familiar pit of depression. I couldn't help but wonder if a little talk with Jesus could've helped me.

"I thanked Him for you, asked Him to help me to always make you happy," he offered.

And for some reason, his speaking in terms of always didn't bother me, even though I'd only just met him.

"Thank you."

"You're welcome, Von. Hey, I'm gonna run to the house and see if I can get us some breakfast. Be right back."

"Wait, I'll go with you," I said. "I need to shower and change."

"Shower here and put on something of mine. I'll be right back."

He kneeled next to the bed, kissed me, and left. I lay there gazing up at the ceiling while simultaneously trying to bait down the giddiness induced by being there in his space. I closed my contented eyes for a bit before climbing out of bed and slowly walking through the small house to the bathroom, where I showered with his black soap and put on a pair of his boxers and one of his t-shirts that was folded neatly on his kitchen table along with other piles of laundry, my thick body filling every inch of fabric. I even put a little of his cologne on my wrist and brushed my barely-there hair with his stiff-bristled palm brush, wondering how effective it was on his thick head of hair. The last thing I did was brush my teeth with my finger and swish with some of his mouthwash.

I made the bed, then sat on it and inspected the bareness of the walls—no pictures, no evidence of his travels or of his past at all. My home, by contrast, was full of memories, but that had been my undoing as I tried to cope with Wade's passing. Maybe August's idea of decor was smarter.

I had just lay back on the bed and was staring at the ceiling again when he arrived with two foil-covered paper plates. We enjoyed a hearty breakfast while sitting on the low steps of his front porch. And afterwards, he sat on a lower step, between my legs, and I greased his scalp.

***

We were lounging under a massive oak tree, watching the day

pass by when I began to speak. Talking to August was easy and something I really felt compelled to do. No one in my life before him had ever really listened to me, except for the therapist in the psych ward and others I had visited off and on throughout my life. There were days I'd wake up sad, and the entire day would pass before I'd snap out of it. I always felt like my feelings or thoughts didn't matter to Evetta or Wade. That was probably because neither of them understood why I was so "sensitive."

I told him about my hard-working but largely absent mother, the father who left us when Evetta and I were girls, and my mother's untimely death. I told him of Evetta's love and care for me, how she'd virtually raised me and put me through college. "She even picked out my major and like I said before, she chose Wade as my boyfriend, urged me to marry him when he proposed."

"You didn't want to marry him?" August asked.

"I wasn't sure what I wanted, other than to make Evetta happy. I always felt like I owed her so much and she'd always done what was best for me, so if she said Wade was the one, I believed her."

"But he wasn't, was he?"

I frowned slightly. "Why do you say that?"

"Your voice when you talk about him. You don't sound like you're talking about a great love."

I sighed. "Well, he was older—my sister's age—and he was stable and a good provider and we lived a good life together in the material sense. He took care of me just like Evetta always had, but..."

"What, Von?" he asked as he wrapped his arm around my shoulder and squeezed.

"He had all these rules about how I was to dress or behave. He was always afraid I'd embarrass him because I wasn't raised like he was, meaning I grew up poor. He was a business man so there were always parties and events to attend, people to entertain and sometimes I enjoyed all of that. But between us there just was no... I don't know."

"There was none of this?" he asked as he softly nibbled my ear, then my neck.

I sucked in a breath and quickly released it. "If you mean passion, no, there was none of that."

With his lips still on my neck, he said, "Hmm, what about kids?"

"We tried for a while and then we gave up. There was nothing wrong medically with either of us. It just never happened. And to be honest, I never really wanted to have kids, not with him."

He backed away a little and nodded as if he totally understood.

"What about you? Why no wife and kids?" I asked.

"Because I just met you."

11
"Could it be I'm Falling in Love"

We had dinner that evening at the big house—August's idea. I honestly would've rather stayed at his little place because there was something peaceful and enchanting about it to me. But I was more than happy that I would be sharing the meal with him, no matter where we ate it.

I rushed upstairs and changed once we made it to the house, with August waiting outside my door for me. He walked me to the dining room where we were greeted by the smiling faces of the women of Hyacinth Manor—Rosa, Dee Dee, Rochelle, and Dorcas. They glanced at each other knowingly when August pulled my chair out for me, sighed when he kissed my cheek. I wouldn't have been surprised if they'd applauded when he fixed my plate for me. Dinner was full of chatter as the women talked about the goings-on in the small, predominantly black town. August sat next to me, held my hand when he could, brushed my thigh with his from time to time. The only thoughts in my head were: how could this man I barely knew make me feel so… so *alive*? Was I falling in love with him this quickly? If not, what *was* this?

"I want to let Von and August in on a little secret. I saw this coming, knew from the moment you walked in the door, Von, that you were his. It's a part of my ministry to know these things," Ms. Rosa said.

"I knew it when I saw her, too," August said, his eyes trained on me.

I blushed.

"That's why you put her in Room Ten?" Rochelle asked.

"Yep. Just trying to help things along."

Seeing my confused expression, August leaned over and said, "Legend has it that anyone who stays in that room is sure to fall in love soon thereafter."

"Oh," I said with a nod.

Rosa said, "I know it probably sounds crazy, but that room hasn't failed yet."

I reached over and grasped August's hand. "I don't think it's crazy at all, and I know for sure this place is special. And that room is the first place I ever saw him—through the window—so that makes it special, too."

***

August gently held me against the blue-striped wallpapered wall outside my door after dinner and kissed me urgently. My head swam as I dug my fingers into his thick hair and let them get tangled in the coils. One of his huge hands rested on my back, the other rested on my cheek, and I just rested in his arms. When he came up for air, I said, "I don't want you to leave me alone tonight."

"I don't intend to," he said.

Inside my room, we kissed our way through the darkness to my bed where we sat side by side, holding each other, mouths bound, hearts intertwined. If this was what love at first sight felt like, I felt sorry for anyone who'd never experienced it.

I broke our connection, caught my breath, and said, "Why couldn't I have met you years ago? Why did I have to wait so long to feel this?"

He smiled, took my hand, and kissed my fingers. "One thing I know about God is that His timing is perfect. We are the right people for each other today. That probably wouldn't have been true years ago. We were different people living different lives then."

"I guess you're right. Well, I'm so glad we're who we are right now. I'm so glad I came here and found you."

"Me, too, baby. Can I call you that?"

"You can call me anything you'd like."

He leaned in to kiss me, but I stopped him and said, "I need to go to the restroom. Be right back."

He pulled his shirt over his head and tossed it to the floor, showing off that chiseled chest of his. "Hurry," he said with a grin.

"I will."

In the bathroom, I stared at myself in the mirror just to see if I was really me, pinched myself to see if maybe I was dreaming. Then I thanked the God I hadn't talked to since I was a girl, when a local church would pick us kids up from the projects and take us to Sunday morning service, for August Donovan. I thanked Him for giving me someone who made my heart race and made my smile brighter than it had ever been before, for giving me what I'd been missing all those years. Then I smiled at myself and exited the bathroom to find the light on and August gone.

12
"Going in Circles"

I waited all night for him to return to my room, to me.

He never did.

After sitting and staring at the door until my vision began to blur, then standing and staring out the window until my legs began to tremble, I paced the floor until fatigue set in and I was forced to climb into bed with confusion dominating my mind and tears infiltrating my eyes. I quickly fell into a troubled sleep which was filled with images of my late husband, Wade, his words angry as he criticized me and belittled me for nothing and for everything, as he would often do. His face danced before me as he shook his head and uttered phrases I'd heard so many times I doubted I'd ever forget them: "You just can't think, can you? There is nothing in that brain of yours, *absolutely nothing*. All you know how to do is screw. That's it! How would you ever survive without me, Von?"

I finally woke up late the next morning, drenched in sweat and with a blindingly throbbing headache. I moaned in pain, realizing this was the first headache I'd had in months. There was once a time that a day without a headache was a rarity for me. I had to drag myself out of bed, trying to shake the disconcerting dreams off while my mind wandered to August. I wondered if I had dreamt the whole thing with him. Maybe I really was crazy, insane even, psychotic. Maybe there was no August at all. Maybe there was no Hyacinth Manor or Hyacinth Valley or Room Ten. Maybe I was back home in my house and had imagined it all. Even worse, maybe I was still in that psych ward suffering from the side effects of the medicine they kept shoving at me.

I stood in the middle of the room and stared at the painting of the woman and wondered if my mind had made that up, too. I shifted my eyes to the luscious green lawn outside the window and shook my head. I hadn't made this place up. It was all real and I was just stupid. That was it. I was stupid to think I'd made some connection with a mysterious handsome man, stupid to think whatever we could possibly have had together could've worked. Stupid to believe he was really attracted to a woman like me, a weakling who could barely wipe her behind without directions.

I thought about trying to have a late breakfast and then decided there was no point in it, and climbed back into bed where I spent the balance of the day.

August never came to me.

The next morning I was too hungry from going an entire twenty-four hours without food to stay holed up in my room, so I put on my robe and schlepped down to breakfast, more than happy to find the dining room empty. Ms. Dorcas peeped out the kitchen door to say hi but that was it. No other human companionship, thank goodness. I returned to my room until lunch, which I also enjoyed in peaceful solitude. My luck ran out at dinnertime when I arrived once again in my robe and was forced to break bread with Rosa, who had put me in that accursed room. Rochelle was there as well.

Their eyes widened upon seeing my condition. I hadn't bathed or changed clothes in a couple of days, and I knew for a fact there were huge bags under my eyes because I had spied them in the bathroom mirror earlier. They tried to engage me in small talk, but soon gave up after seeing I would only grunt in response.

The next day brought more of the same.

By the fourth day I was no longer depressed, I was mad as hell. He had made the first move, claimed he prayed for me, and then, right when I was poised and ready to give him my goodies, he bailed on me. I woke up that morning with a determination to give August Donovan a piece of my mind, and then I intended to pack my bags, settle what was sure to be an enormous bill with Rosa, and leave and go somewhere, anywhere but Hyacinth Manor.

Fueled by anger, I hopped out of bed, showered and dressed, went down for a quick breakfast, and immediately left the house, stomping past the bushes and the beds of flowers that shared their name with the town and manor, bound for August's cabin.

It didn't take me long to get there. I tried the door to find it locked, and then began to pound on it. Pain shot through my fists as they hit the heavy wood, but that physical pain felt better than the mental anguish I'd endured over the past few days and for most of my life.

"August, it's Von. Open this door or I'm going to find a big rock out here and break a window and let myself in!"

The lock on the front door disengaged almost immediately, and then the door creaked open to reveal a bedraggled-looking August on the other side. He scratched his beard and stepped to the side, allowing me into the living-combination-bedroom.

Before I could say a word, he pulled me to him and held me tightly, whispered, "I'm sorry, baby," in my ear.

I wasn't expecting that.

I was supposed to give him a peace of my mind, cuss him out, *something*. Then I was supposed to leave him in my dust. But his arms were around me and his breath was on my ear and I just couldn't do any of those things. He'd messed up my well-thought-out plans.

"I should've come to you, explained myself. I'm so sorry."

I gathered some strength and backed out of his arms. "What happened?" I asked softly, my anger nearly a distant memory.

"The painting."

I frowned. "What painting?"

He sighed and reached for my hand. "Come with me."

I took his hand out of a combination of curiosity and what I was fast coming to grips with as being the opening notes of love. That had to be what was unfolding in my heart. What else could explain how relieved I was when he opened that door, despite how angry I was at the same time? I followed him through the small living room, and the smaller kitchen to the closed door of the bedroom. He released my hand, pulled out a key, and unceremoniously unlocked and opened the door. My jaw dropped as my eyes took in the contents of the room.

Sitting on the floor against the walls was canvas after canvas of beautiful artwork in different stages of completion. Portraits of brown people in all shades, young and old. I stepped forward and crouched in front of one canvas, and gently touched the brush-stroked face of a distinguished-looking older man. There were others lined behind it, so many piles of art, all of which looked to have been created with loving care. Containers of paint and a mound of different-sized brushes covered the floor in the center of the room. I looked up at him. "You painted these? All of these?"

He nodded soberly.

"They're beautiful, August. I've never seen anything as beautiful as these paintings. Except—the one in my room, that's yours too, isn't it?" I asked as my eyes glimpsed the familiar scribbled signature on the painting.

He nodded again.

"I don't understand. Why would you hide these, keep them locked up?"

"Because of what they represent."

I stood and walked over to him. "I don't know what they could represent other than the most talent I have ever seen in my entire life, and I've been to tons of galleries and gallery openings and art showings. I just do not understand why you would hide these."

He slid the fingers of his hand through mine and tugged, pulling me out of the room and closing the door behind me, locking it again. He led me into the living room, sat on the bed, and then pulled me onto his lap, gathering me in his arms and holding me tightly. "I was living in New York before I came back here. My last memory of living there was waking up in a place I still can't remember going to.

I was lying on a floor in a pile of my own vomit and there was a syringe on the floor next to me," he said into my ear.

I tried to pull away a bit so I could see his face, but he wouldn't loosen his grip.

"I'd been on drugs for a while by then, had tried anything you can name and some other things you've probably never heard of, and it all started with my art."

"August—"

"I was discovered, if you want to call it that, when I was twenty-six. I was living in Los Angeles then, had done a few large commissions, but I paid my rent by doing quick little portraits of tourists in different spots throughout the city. One of those tourists was rich, loved my work, and became my benefactor. He paid for me to travel the country showing my work in different cities. Then there were the trips overseas. Then celebrities began to commission my work. There was so much money; so many people loved and respected what I was doing. There were parties, too, so many parties. For a while it was like living a dream, Von." He stopped and sighed. "There were always drugs at the parties I was invited to. Drugs, women, anything you can imagine. Things that can undo a young black man from rural Arkansas, but I didn't give in to any of it at first and when I did indulge, I only did so socially.

"But Von, success can be just as hard on you as failure. There was so much pressure to *stay* successful, and I didn't have anyone I could talk to, no one to help keep me grounded, or at least no one who would understand. My mom just saw all the money I was sending her and she thought any complaining I did was silly. My friends were the same way.

"Von, it got to the place where I couldn't paint. All of the pressure had me creatively bankrupt. I just couldn't create anything worth selling. The worst feeling in the world is being able to make magic and then waking up one day to find that you can't anymore. So I turned to drugs and alcohol and women as a way of coping. I had done those things recreationally before, but they became compulsions for me, *addictions*.

"To top it all off, no one wanted to buy the stuff I created right before the pressure got to me because they didn't want to deal with someone who was an obvious junkie, since I had begun to look the part.

"I spiraled out of control. Spent more money than I could keep track of. Von, I'm not talking about a few months, I was strung out for years, *years*. My mom died and I was high at her funeral. I was high all day, every day, until I woke up one morning and saw where I was and what I had become. I prayed right then and there because I knew if I kept that up I was going to die and end up being a byword, as the Bible would put it. I prayed hard, Von, and the only thing God told me was to go home. That was three years ago. I got on a plane the next day and came straight here because I knew Ms. Rosa would help me. Went through withdrawals in the big house, right there in Room Ten. I don't know why it took me so long to fall in love. I told Ms. Rosa that room must not work on men."

I smiled.

"Ms. Rosa helped me through it all. Only payment she wanted was a painting, so I gave the one that's hanging in that room right now. The woman in the painting was my lover for a while, one among many I had over the years."

"Did you love her, the woman in the picture?" I asked and then I felt silly that after all he'd just told me, that was the only thing in my mind.

"You are the first woman I have ever loved, Von."

Tears crowded my eyes. "You really love me? I mean, *really*?"

"From the bottom of my heart."

I let the tears fall as he loosened his grip and held my face in his hands. "Like I said before, I knew you were mine the moment I laid eyes on you."

I smiled. "You sure you weren't influenced by Ms. Rosa a little?"

"All she did was tell me we had a new guest. She didn't tell me that guest was my other half, *my rib*. Von, I loved the idea of you long before I met you. You're my soul mate, my heartbeat."

I leaned in and kissed him, then he continued with his story. "I had most of the artwork in the bedroom shipped here when I left New York, the remnants of the time when I could still paint. Some I would paint on the odd sober day here and there, too. I hadn't painted in years, not since I got here. Hadn't even wanted to until I laid eyes on you." He slid me off of his lap onto the bed and stood to his feet. "Stay here, I want to show you something."

I nodded and wiped my wet cheeks. He returned a few minutes later with a canvas in his hand, the back of it turned to me. "I hadn't stepped foot in that room, your room, in so long, I'd forgotten the painting was even there and when I saw it—"

"That's why you left the other night? The painting?"

He nodded. "It brought back memories I wasn't ready to deal with, reminded me of who I was and who I could become again, made me feel like I wasn't fit to love you, Von. So yeah, I ran away from you, but you found me."

I gave him a little smile. "It wasn't hard since I know where you live."

"I don't mean today. You... you never left my thoughts. I kept seeing you here, in my clothes, in my bed. So—" He flipped the canvas around. "I painted you. The first work I've completed in a very long time."

I stared at the painting, placed my hand over my heart, and gasped. He'd captured every line of my face, every curve of my body—me, in repose—and I was *beautiful*. I looked up at him— speechless.

"I finished it yesterday. Do you like it?"

"You made me look *so beautiful*. Yes, I like it—I *love* it!"

"You *are* beautiful, Von." He leaned the painting against the wall. "Will you be patient with me? I'm sorry for running."

"Don't run from me again, please."

"I won't. I promise."

"Um, August," I said shyly, "can we finish what we started the other night?"

He sat down next to me and took my hand in his. "When the time is right, we can. I was moving too fast and almost stepped outside the bounds of what I know to be right. I'm sorry about that, too. You just have a profound effect on me, Von. But look, let's just take our time and do this right. Take the vows before we start doing things that belong in the confines of the covenant."

I was a little disappointed, but I nodded and said, "Okay... August, I'm sorry you went through so much pain."

"I'm not. It was good for me to be afflicted so that I might learn *His* decrees," he said, pointing to the sky.

We sat in comfortable silence for several minutes before I said, "What do we do now?"

"We keep courting, baby," he said before kissing my breath away.

13
"Free"

For two glorious weeks, August's face was the first one I saw in the morning and the last one I saw before I closed my eyes at night. I stayed with him in his little house and we talked and laughed, ate and slept, prayed together. We danced to his old Temptations and Four Tops and Chaka Khan and Rufus albums—he loved music so much, he often let it play as we drifted off to sleep at night. He talked about his former life, his travels, promised to show me the world one day. I told him the cabin was world enough for me. He asked me about my hopes and dreams. I told him I was living my dream by being with someone like him, someone who treated me like I'd never been treated before—with respect and kindness. Though I hadn't told him so, I loved him—beard, messy hair, handsome face, and all. I loved his smile, loved his voice. Loved sleeping in his arms and feeling his heartbeat. I loved the quiet and solitude of his little house out in the middle of the woods. I loved that he didn't have a phone or a TV or even a car. I loved that he didn't have a computer or emails to check or a job that was more important than me or business meetings that kept him away from me. I loved that being with him didn't mean I had to wear make-up or straighten my hair or host or attend dinner parties and smile and pretend to like people I didn't like. I loved that my sister couldn't swoop in and ruin us.

My sister.

I hadn't talked to her in weeks. As a matter of fact, she honestly hadn't crossed my mind and I felt guilty about that, realizing she must have been worried half out of her mind about me. So one day, while August was doing some work around the big house, I returned to my abandoned room and charged up my long-dead cell phone. Then I dialed my sister's number and held my breath.

"Von?" she said softly this time instead of screaming in my ear.

"Yeah. Just calling to let you know I'm okay. I'm doing good."

"Well, isn't that nice? I suppose you're still not going to tell me where you are?"

"There's no need to."

"What did I do to you other than sacrifice my entire life for you, Von? What did I do to cause you to run away and make me worry like this?"

I leaned forward on the sofa and rubbed my forehead. I felt a headache coming on. "Don't you think you're exaggerating a little, Evetta? I was with Wade for more than twenty years. So you really haven't sacrificed your entire life."

"You were with him because of me!"

"You still think that's something to brag about?"

"I picked you a husband who took excellent care of you, gave you everything a woman could dream of, so yes, I think it's something to brag about."

"He gave me everything but real love."

"I can't believe you are on this phone speaking ill of the dead. I taught you better than that, little sister."

"You also taught me to tell the truth. Wade was a great provider but a terrible husband."

"This is about Wade? That's why you've run away?"

"It's about me needing and wanting to be happy for once, Evetta. And right now I am very happy."

There was a moment of silence before she said, "There's a man, isn't there?"

I held the phone.

"There is! That explains it. You ran off with some man, probably some good-for-nothing who is going to rob you blind of all Wade left you. You need to come home right now! You have that big house just sitting over there waiting for you. Come home, Von. I'll help you find another husband, a proper one, someone who can take care of you."

I released a frustrated sigh, felt the headache begin to intensify.

"I gotta go, Evetta. I'll call back soon."

I ended the call without waiting for her reply and almost simultaneously, a knock came at the door. I laid the phone on the sofa and could hear it vibrating as I went to answer the door—most assuredly it was Evetta calling back.

A relieved smile spread across my face at the sight on the other side. As soon as he saw me, August pulled me into his arms and I followed him back to our little love nest in the woods. My headache had disappeared.

**

August and I lay on our backs in his bed, enjoying his new window unit air conditioner and listening to an old James Cleveland album of his because it was just too hot to do anything else. "I don't know how you've survived this long without air conditioning," I said as I rolled over to face him.

He chuckled. "I guess I just got used to it."

"It's amazing that your artwork hasn't melted or something."

"That room is shaded by trees so it stays pretty cool."

I rested my head on his chest. "I never want to leave you."

"You never have to."

After a few minutes of silence, I summoned the courage to say, "There's something I need to tell you."

He left the bed, turned the music off, and then rejoined me, taking me into his arms. "What is it, Von? You can tell me anything."

I played with the hair of his chest for a few minutes before saying, "I have a history of depression."

He shrugged. "Well, your husband died, so I can understand that."

"No, it started well before I even met him, when I was a child. I had trouble coping with things and no one to really help me because I was essentially being raised by a child—this is hard for me, August."

"Take your time, baby, we've got plenty of it."

I sighed lightly, adjusted my head on his chest. "I've been on and off of medicine for years—antidepressants. I-uh, had a bad breakdown and was admitted to a psych ward shortly before I came here. I feel better now, I really do, but I'm not going to pretend I will never be depressed again. It's been a part of me for a long time. I... I just wanted you to know and I understand if you don't want to be with me anymore. Oh, and my name is really LaVonda. LaVonda Ingram. Von is my nickname."

August sat up in bed and looked me in the eye. "Well, I prefer Von and listen, if you are willing to be with a drug addict who will always have to fight to stay clean, I am willing to love you through your depression and not just today, but for the rest of our lives. We're gonna pray, baby, and we're gonna love, and if either of us feels weak, we're gonna get whatever help we need and lean on our God. What you just told me doesn't scare me, it makes me love you more, it explains our connection. God has taken all of our broken pieces, baby, and put them together again so we'll be whole for each other."

My heart was so full, I could only utter four little words: "I love you, August."

"Almost as much as I love you."

14
"Don't Mess With My Man"

"Ms. Dorcas says a new guest checked in last night," August said as he walked into the cabin with our breakfast in hand. This was the first guest other than me to arrive in the month or so I'd been there.

"Really? Were they invited or did Ms. Rosa bend the rules for them, too?"

August smiled as he handed me my plate. "Let me let you in on a little secret. Ms. Rosa only had that put on the sign to ward off white people. When she bought the place, she was determined that no white folks would be served there ever again. Saying it's an invitation-only establishment keeps her out of legal trouble."

"I see her point, but don't you think that's a little reverse racism?"

"I think maybe she experienced enough racism in her lifetime not to care."

"How in the world does she keep this place open, though? I mean, as far as I've seen, it is anything but busy."

"This place is important to a lot of people. So many have fallen in love here, gotten married here, it's important to them that the manor stays open so she gets monthly donations, monetary gifts that keep her afloat, and her son helps her out, too."

"I see. That's wonderful. So, what did she do before she bought this place?" I asked as I peeled the foil back on my plate.

"She was a teacher. Hey, I think you should bring your stuff here. No sense in leaving it in that room when you're here all the time."

I shoved a piece of bacon into my mouth and nodded in agreement. "Okay." There was no place I'd have rather been than right where I was.

**

That evening, August and I walked hand-in-hand to dinner and once we arrived, my stomach dropped. Sitting at the table was my sister. I wanted to either break and run away, or hide behind August. But she saw me as soon as I entered the room, so there was no sense in running or hiding. And then I told myself that Evetta was my sister, a human woman, and not the big bad wolf. There was no reason for me to want to break and run away from her at all.

She looked just as she always did—expensive make-up, expensive weave, expensive clothes, air of superiority.

I followed August to our regular side of the table, sat down in the chair he pulled out for me, barely felt his kiss on my cheek, didn't respond when the other ladies at the table spoke to me. My eyes were glued to my sister who sat directly across the table from me with angry, disappointed eyes, eyes so much like mine, fixed on me.

"There you are," she said. "You look a mess, but at least your hair is growing back. You don't look like a Marine anymore. I should've known you were losing it when you started having all of that beautiful hair of yours hacked off. You looked ridiculous at Wade's funeral." Sweet, compassionate Evetta was long gone, probably left when I absconded without her permission. Impatient, domineering

Evetta, the Evetta I was most familiar with, was here.

"How did you find me?" I asked as August set my plate before me.

"Had your phone tracked after you finally left it on for more than a minute."

"I'm not going back with you," I said as August sat down next to me and rested his hand on my thigh. I knew he and everyone else had to be confused, but I could only deal with one person at a time.

"You're not staying here with *him*. He looks like a mountain man for goodness' sake."

"His name is August."

"Well, I'm sure *August* can't take care of you. Looks like he cuts trees for a living."

"He's an artist, a brilliant one."

"That's worse! LaVonda Shay Carter-Ingram, you will pack your things and leave with me first thing in the morning. We are not going to argue about this."

"She said she's staying," August said.

Her head snapped in his direction. "This is between me and my sister. You can stay out of it."

"No, this is between you and my woman. If she wants to stay, she stays."

She leaned back in her chair and chuckled bitterly. "He's gonna bleed you dry."

"I don't believe he will, but honestly, I couldn't care less about Wade's money, Evetta."

"It's *your* money now and I don't *believe* this. You should still be in mourning, not laying up with some unshaven bum!"

"First of all, you really need to keep your mouth off of my man. Second—mourning? What the hell is there to mourn, Evetta? The fact that the man who treated me like I had no brain and belittled me for most of my life is dead, or the fact that he took his own life, or the fact that he took his mistress's life first? Huh? Because the only thing I've been really sad about is the fact that I faithfully sat around and let him treat me like dog crap for twenty-plus years for some unknown and unfathomable reason, and he not only cheated on me but with my so-called friend and then decided he'd rather die than be without her. Twenty years of marriage, Evetta, not to mention the years I shacked up with him before. *Twenty years* and he left me in shame!"

I think just about everyone's mouths dropped open except for mine and Evetta's.

"You don't know if that's really what happened. Maybe—"

"I found letters, Evetta. And so did her husband. We compared them. Plus, he did it at her job. There are *several* witnesses! What I said is exactly what happened. She tried to break things off and he couldn't take it. So your first-round pick was a cheater and a horrible person who treated me like I was crazy long before I was and made my life hell, so excuse me if I no longer trust your assessment of people. I'm not leaving. I'm right where I want and need to be. So you can go back to your husband and live your life and let me live mine with my man." I glanced up to see a slight grin on Rosa's face and I thought I heard Rochelle say, "Umph, I heard that."

"As my cousin Anita Baker would say, you better watch your step," Dee Dee muttered.

August leaned in and kissed my cheek, rubbed my back.

"You've forgotten one thing: I have power of attorney over you. I will have you committed in a heartbeat, because you have obviously lost your mind. I mean, you've never been much of a thinker, but this is utterly insane! So you can leave in the car with me or in the back of an ambulance. Your choice," she said with one eyebrow cocked up.

I stood from the table and leaned across it, bringing my face closer to hers. "You do whatever you are big and bad enough to do. But understand this, if you try to have me committed, you are no longer my sister, you will be as good as dead to me, and once I prove my sanity, I will sue the pants off of you and Dan. Your asses will be homeless when I'm done. I'll wipe my butt with the money right in your face, too."

Her eyes widened in shock. Evetta lived for her house and her granite countertops and intricate recessed lighting. She was all about status and even the hint of a drop in hers would induce a nervous breakdown.

I reached for August's hand. "Now I'm leaving with him and when I get to his place, I'm gonna strip and climb into his bed and we're gonna have wild, mountain man sex and I'm gonna scream loud enough for you to hear." I turned my attention to the other ladies at the table. "Sorry for getting graphic in front of you ladies. I meant no disrespect."

"None taken," Rosa and Rochelle said, almost in unison.

"Lord, I think I'ma go call Farris now and renegotiate some things," Dorcas said, fanning herself with a napkin. "It just got hot up in here!"

Dee Dee covered her mouth but failed at stifling her laughter.

As August and I walked the trail back to his house, he said, "You and your sister look very similar, you really resemble each other."

"Same parents."

"But you are so different otherwise."

"I know."

We walked a few paces and then he cleared his throat. "Um... mountain man sex?"

I blushed. "Sorry about that. I know we're waiting, but I had to say it. She deserved it."

"I don't know her, but she definitely deserves something for treating you like that. If she's not careful, she'll get it, too."

"You're probably right. You know, I have never spoken to her like that before, but it felt..."

"Good?"

"Very."

Evetta left the next morning.

15
"Happy"

"I'm sorry about what happened with your husband," August said early one morning, about a week after Evetta left. We were still in bed. The sun had barely risen.

"I should've told you before. I just don't like talking about it."

"I can understand why."

"It hurt, August. I mean, it happened on our anniversary. I had just finished cooking dinner for us when I got the call. He went to her job, told her if he couldn't have her, no one could, killed her in front of her co-workers. Then he shot himself."

"Von..."

"I did care about him despite how he treated me—the... the emotional abuse—and it hurt to know he loved another woman, someone I'd broken bread with and considered a friend, so much he was willing to take his own life and leave me behind. And those letters... those letters just broke my heart. Declarations of love he'd never made to me. It made me feel like a fool for ever marrying him and *staying* married to him."

"Made you resent your sister, too?"

"A little." I sighed. "Me and Evetta have a complicated relationship. I love her for always taking care of me, hate her for always trying to control me. I know she loves me, she just has a warped view of some things."

"That, she does."

"And I'm sorry she said those things about you."

"Yeah, well, you didn't say them so her words don't matter."

"Thank you for understanding."

"Thank you for letting me love you."

"I wouldn't have it any other way."

"Mmm. Hey, you want to use that car of yours and go do something fun?"

"As long as I'm with you, yes. What do you have in mind?"

"It's a surprise. Just get dressed. We'll leave after breakfast."

"Get dressed in what?"

"Something cool and comfortable."

August gassed up my car in town then came back and picked me up. As he sped down the highway towards my surprise, I tried unsuccessfully not to stare at him. He'd dressed in his signature way—jeans that fit his long body perfectly and a crisp white t-shirt. His thick, long, kinky hair was just as wild as ever, and the untrimmed beard and mustache I loved still adorned his handsome face.

"Whatchu looking at?" he asked.

"Hmm, I think I'm looking at the love of my life."

"So you finally figured that out, huh?"

I rolled my eyes and rested my head against the headrest. Before I knew it, the ride had lulled me to sleep.

***

"Wake up, baby. We're here," August said a couple of hours later.

I opened my eyes and sat up straight in my seat, a little disoriented but happy it was his voice that had awakened me.

"Where's here?" I asked through a yawn.

"The Altheimer Blues Fest at the Cook Family Park."

"We're in Altheimer, Arkansas?"

"Yep."

I frowned slightly and took in our surroundings as he rolled his window down to pay for our entry into the event. All I could see around us besides the line of cars entering the gate were lonely stretches of highway and towering trees. Upon entering the park—which was really just a freshly-cut open field with a stage set up at one end—I smiled, remembering August's love for music and though I wasn't the biggest blues fan, something told me I was in for a good time. Well, the fact that I was with August told me that, actually.

We exited my car and he took my hand and led me past groups of boisterous black folk in lawn chairs, nursing cans of beer or soda, some of them with umbrellas over their heads, most of them with bulging ice chests at their feet. The delicious aroma of barbecue smoke filled the air, teasing my belly. I smiled at the laughter and the lazy drum beat and whining guitar-laden blues streaming from the speakers onstage as the growing crowd gathered in the park.

"We didn't bring chairs," I said as we made our way closer to the stage.

"We don't need any," he replied with a grin.

We reached a ringed-off area of tables and chairs situated in the grass directly in front of the stage. August and the huge man who was blocking the entrance to that section greeted each other loudly, shook hands, and gave each other a brother hug. "Von, this is an old friend of mine, Tyrone. 'Rone, this is my lady, Von."

"Nice to meet you, Ms. Von. Man, I don't know what this fine lady wants with you," Tyrone said with a smile.

"Stop hating. Where's Dianne?"

"Over by the picture booth."

"I can't believe you guys are still together. She hasn't divorced you yet?"

"You know she can't resist your boy. Hey, she's got barbecue sandwiches and turkey legs for sale over there and she's been asking about you so make sure you holler at her."

They gripped hands again and August said, "Most definitely."

Tyrone moved to the side and August led me to one of the smaller tables. "Welcome to VIP, baby."

I was grinning from ear to ear as I took my seat.

August leaned over and kissed me before leaving to grab us some drinks and food. I took the time he was away to check out the crowd—couples and groups could be seen laughing and talking in anticipation of what I assumed would be a day-long event. Wade wouldn't have been caught dead at an event like this, but it seemed fun to me. I'd often wanted to attend a music festival of some sort.

The women in attendance had their hair laid and I could tell they were wearing new or nearly new outfits with fingernails and toenails painted to match. Their faces were made up like they were attending a fashion show, rather than a blues fest in the middle of a hot Arkansas summer. I actually felt a little underdressed but at the same time, August and I were perfectly coordinated as he was definitely a no-frills man.

"Hey, I just wanted to say how good it is to meet you," a voice said from out of nowhere, startling me.

I looked up to see that it was Tyrone. He sank his giant body into the folding chair next to mine and added, "I can tell you're making my boy happy and he deserves it."

"Well, he's definitely making me happy, too."

"Good. Hold onto him, he's good people. We grew up together, he's always been one of the good guys."

"Oh, I have no plans of letting him go."

He stood from the chair just as August returned with an armload of food and drinks. "'Rone, you're my boy, but if I find out you been hitting on my woman, Dianne and I both are gonna whoop your ass."

Tyrone raised his meaty hands and shook his head. "Naw, Dianne would *kill* me," he said and they both laughed. "Y'all enjoy the show, man. It's a good line up."

"Thanks, 'Rone." He turned to me and said, "I got sodas and water, a couple of brisket sandwiches, some ribs, potato salad, oh, and a turkey leg."

"Wow," I said as I stared at the spread in front of me.

He sat down beside me and placed his arm around my shoulder. "Now, let me give you the lay of the land. The ladies' room is right over there," he said, pointing to a set of bright blue Porta-Potties at the far end of the field.

I giggled lightly. "Good to know."

"The show starts in a few minutes with a local act so just sit back and relax." He kissed me. "Oh, and I have some Off spray and a couple of towels in my backpack."

"Okay," I said. I'd forgotten he brought a backpack with him.

"LaVonda Ingram?" asked a female voice loudly.

The voice sounded familiar but I had no idea where it came from. My eyes scanned the crowd and fell on a smiling face from my past sitting a table away from us. "Paula?" I asked. I couldn't believe my eyes. Paula Frazier was the ring leader of the executive wives' club I inadvertently joined upon marrying Wade. She hosted the best parties in her palatial suburban home, only wore the most expensive clothes, jewelry, and human hair weave. Drove her two kids to private school in a Range Rover Autobiography, vacationed in Europe with her much older husband, Garvin.

"Yes!" she shrieked as she stood from her table and made her way over to ours. I couldn't help but notice that the man at the table with her was *not* Garvin Frazier. I stood to meet her, let her pull me into an overly enthusiastic hug. We'd been friends out of proximity, not choice. "I thought that was you! Girl, that haircut is everything! You look positively radiant!" she gushed.

I rubbed my hand over my hair which had grown from a buzz cut to a small afro in the time I'd been in Hyacinth Valley. "Thanks. Um, I'm surprised to see you here," I said, my eyes darting back toward her table mate.

"Yeah, I guess it *is* surprising, but that's what a new man and a new life will do to you."

"You and Garvin split?" I said before I could stop myself.

"Mm-hmm. I was so tired of being his arm candy, just another one of his possessions, and I couldn't take any more of his rampant cheating. So I divorced him, got awarded plenty of alimony and child support and I got to keep the house…" She glanced back at her table. "And the pool guy." She giggled and slapped me on the arm.

I smiled at the gorgeous, dark-skinned specimen sitting at her table. "Wow… well, good for you."

"Thanks! And I see you've moved on." She gave August a little smile.

"Oh," I said. "August, this is Paula, an old friend of mine. Paula, this is August."

She gave him a sweet "hello," then leaned in close to my ear and said, "Excuse my French, but let me go back to the hood where I grew up and say, damn! Where you find him at?"

I wagged my finger at her. "I'll never tell."

"I don't blame you. Well, dear, he is definitely good for you. In all the years I've known you, I've never seen you look so good. I always thought you were the saddest person I'd ever met. I'm happy for you."

"Thanks."

"Well, enjoy the show. I know I will." And with that, she flounced back to her table and fell right into the pool guy's lap with a loud giggle. This was not the well put together, poised Paula Frazier from my former life.

"Who'd have thought it?" I said softly. "Paula Frazier letting loose and having fun at a blues fest."

"She just might be thinking the same thing about you," August said. And he was probably right. Fun was not a word I would've associated with my former self or my former life.

And I did let loose and have fun.

We ate, guzzled sodas, and kissed off and on through the first act which was good but not spectacular. As the day drew on, the acts got progressively better. By the time the sun set, Bigg Robb was onstage singing about the "Sugar Shack," and August and I two-stepped in the tiny space next to our table. We watched the acts, ate more food, drank more drinks, swayed to the music, laughed and talked, sprayed Off on our arms and legs to ward off mosquitoes, wiped sweat with the towels he brought, and hugged and kissed all the way through the end of the headliner's—Arkansas's own Bobby Rush—raunchy act. I told August I felt like I needed to repent and wash out my ears after listening to "Booga Bear."

"I thought you were a Christian," I yelled in his ear as an elderly Bobby Rush seized the stage.

"I never said I was perfect," he yelled back and then flashed me a grin.

I could not remember the last time I had that much fun. Well, that was because I'd never had that much fun in my life.

We spent the night in a hotel in Pine Bluff, which was only a few miles from Altheimer. I was sure I was getting lucky because I had never heard of a man who could resist having hotel sex and I knew he had to be ready after hearing all of that very secular music.

So as I sat in the car waiting for him to get our room, I thought about what I was sure was about to happen and by the time he returned to the car and climbed into the driver's seat, my body was dangerously close to overheating. When he grabbed my hand and led me to the room, it was all I could do not to jump him right there in the hallway. And when we reached the door, I lost all control, pushed him against the wall, and nearly ripped his shirt off as I kissed him while wrapping one leg around his waist. Once we parted he said, "Damn... um... baby..."

I nibbled on his neck.

He moaned softly, then I felt him gently push against my shoulders. He held a key card out and said, "Um, here's the key to your room. Mine's right next door."

The hell?

"Are you serious?" I asked.

"Very."

"So you don't wanna do it?"

"I'd have to be dead to not wanna do it. *Of course* I wanna do it, especially after what you just did. It's taking all the strength in me *not* to do it, but we have to wait."

I stared at him for a second or two in disbelief before unlocking my door, walking inside, and slamming it in his face without saying good night.

16
"After the Dance"

"You still mad at me? I see you over there pouting," August said as we headed back to Hyacinth Valley.

I rolled my eyes. "I'm not pouting."

"Yes, you are. Come on, Von, it's not like you didn't know where I stood on the subject."

"Yes, I knew you wanted to wait, but then you took me to a show where the singers specialized in raunchy lyrics. All I heard all day was "do this to me" or "let me do that to you" or "let's do it together." I mean, '*Booga Bear*?' And I don't even want to think about 'Sue.' *And* let's not forget how fine you are. How was I supposed to react?"

He chuckled lightly. "You're right, I *am* fine."

I rolled my eyes again and shifted in the seat so my back was facing him.

"I love you, Von," he said sweetly.

"I hate you."

"No, you don't."

I sure didn't.

He reached over and rubbed my back.

I wanted to snatch away but couldn't.

"Okay, okay, I'm sorry. Maybe I had a lapse in judgment about the music, but I just wanted to show you a good time. You did have a good time other than... *you know*, didn't you?"

I sighed, faced forward in the seat again. "Yes…"

"Really?"

"Yes, *really.*"

"Good."

I glanced over at him and then clasped my hands in my lap. "Look, I'm sorry for the way I acted last night. I guess I don't handle disappointment well, but thank you for everything, and I wanted to tell you that the next time we do something like this, I'm paying. I hate that you spent so much money on gas and food and the hotel rooms."

August didn't say a word but deftly pulled the car from the highway to the shoulder, before fixing his chocolate eyes on me. "Now why in the world would I let you do that?"

"Well, it wasn't fair for you to spend all that money when I have plenty of it just sitting in the bank."

He sat there for a moment, staring at me pensively, then he said, "You think I'm broke."

"What?" I said. That was exactly what I thought.

"You think I'm broke."

I dropped my eyes. "Well, you said—"

"I said I spent more money than I could keep track of on drugs, a ridiculous amount of money, but not *all* of my money. I made a lot of good deals before I went off the deep end. My art has been reproduced on a lot of merchandise—mugs, greeting cards, prints, you name it. I've got plenty of money, too, Von. I live the way I live by choice, not because I'm poor."

I glanced at him and in a timid voice, uttered, "Sorry, I just assumed—sorry."

He reached over and rested his hand on my arm. "Nothing to be sorry for. I guess I sort of misled you, but I'm a man, baby, and as long as I'm *your* man I'm not letting you pay my way or yours either, okay?"

"Okay."

***

We made it back to the manor a few hours later. I was stiff and tired from the ride, and couldn't wait to get back to August's cabin and crawl into his bed. Once we'd climbed out of my car, he wrapped his arm around my waist and kissed my cheek. "It's too late for lunch and too early for dinner, but let's see if Ms. Dorcas will hook us up with something. We're running out of food at home and I'm too tired to walk into town to get something right now."

"You could use my car," I said.

"Thanks for the offer, but I like the walk. I do my best thinking on long walks. Besides, if I spend any more time in that car, I might feel like I've re-entered modern civilization. I'm not trying to do that."

"Well, we've gotta get some real groceries soon so I can cook for you. I'm pretty good, you know?"

He gazed down at me with a glint in his eyes. "Hmm, I bet you are."

I blushed.

As we walked toward the house from the small parking lot on the side, I caught a sight that made me frown—a car.

My *sister's* car.

I didn't panic or want to run. No, I wanted to rush inside the house and cuss her out for having the audacity to come back here and start some more mess with me.

"What's wrong?" August asked.

It was then that I realized I had stopped dead in my tracks and was staring at the car. "That's my sister's car."

"How can you be sure?"

He had a valid point. Tons of people drove Chrysler 300's, and black was a common color for any car. My late husband even drove one at one point. Evetta decided she had to have one after seeing his.

I walked over to the car and checked the plate. It read: *The Mrs*. It was definitely her car. So I stomped to the house, stormed inside, and found myself face to face with my late husband.

17
"You, Me and He"

"Von, Evetta sent me," he said.

I stood frozen in place as I told myself to breathe. I would never get used to this, to seeing his face after his death. "Why?" I asked as August stepped behind me and placed his hands protectively on my shoulders.

Dan, my husband's twin who also happened to be my sister's spouse, said, "She needs you, she's sick."

I shook my head. "I'm not falling for that."

He eyed August and said, "She's really sick. It's not a trick, Von. She's in the ICU."

"She's just trying to lure me back home so she can throw me in some loony bin and have them pump me full of drugs so she can control me."

He somberly shook his head. "I almost wish that was the truth. She had a stroke. She's paralyzed on one side."

I stared at him, tried to read his face, but if he was anything like his late brother, I'd never know if he was lying. "Tell her it was a nice try, but I'm not coming back," I said and then turned to August and added, "Come on, let's go get something to eat."

He took my hand and led me to the kitchen as Dan called after me.

***

"His twin? Your sister fixed you up with her husband's twin?"

I nodded, rested my head on August's shoulder as we sat side by side on his steps awaiting the sunset.

"That's kind of weird, baby."

"I know. But she thought it was neat. And the Ingram brothers were smart and ambitious. She figured us Carter sisters would both be well taken care of, and she was right. Neither of us has had to work a day in our lives."

"It's all about the bottom line with her, huh? *Money*."

"I think she just never wanted either of us to have to work as hard as our mother did. She literally worked herself to death because our father left and never paid a dime of child support."

"I can see that, but it seems like having money is her main focus. Seems like she doesn't care about much else."

"Well, she doesn't care about much else except for trying to run my life."

As the sunlight finally began to dissipate, August said, "You really think she was trying to trick you? You really don't think she's sick."

I stared at the thick trees in front of the cabin and said, "I don't know."

18
"Neither One of Us"

I probably didn't sleep more than an hour in total that night. Dreams, nightmares kept invading my sleep, filling my mind with images of Evetta in a hospital bed connected to machines, or Evetta with a white sheet pulled over her head, or Evetta in a coffin. When I finally rose the next morning, my head was throbbing and my thoughts were muddled. The troubling dreams and lack of sound sleep had put my head in a fog.

"You all right, Von?" August asked as he watched me play with my breakfast. We were in the dining room at the big house.

I sighed and shook my head. "No."

"You're worried about your sister?"

"Yeah."

"You wanna go see about her?"

"Yes. I… I would hate for her to actually be sick and I not go and see about her. She's always been there for me. I owe it to her."

He reached for my hand, squeezed it in his. "Don't go just to repay a debt. Go for love. Love is the only good reason to do anything, Von."

"I do love her, August. She's my sister."

"Then go. I'll be here; I'll wait for you. Just promise you'll come back."

"I will. I have to. I don't even know how long I'll be able to make it without you."

"I don't know what I'm gonna do without *you*."

After a moment of silence, he said, "When we get back to my place, I'll help you get ready. Call Ms. Rosa when you make it there. I'll hang around so I can talk to you. I wanna know how she's doing."

"Okay. August?"

"Yeah, baby?"

"I love you."

"I love you, too."

***

Later that morning, I packed my bags, said my goodbyes to the women of Hyacinth Manor, and once again attempted to pay Ms. Rosa for the time I spent in Room Ten.

Her reply? "You can pay me when you come back."

August put my bags in my trunk and then pulled me tightly into his arms. I could tell he felt apprehensive about me leaving, although he was trying to be supportive.

"You don't want me to go, do you?" I asked.

"Of course not. Who would want to part with a piece of their soul? But I know this is something you need to do. I understand. I just wish there was another way."

"You could come with me."

"If I did, she'd probably have *another* stroke. No, I think this is a journey you have to take alone."

I closed my eyes, breathed in his heady scent, and fought back tears. "I'm coming back as soon as I can."

"Hurry, baby," he whispered.

That's when I broke down and cried into his chest for a full ten minutes or so. Then I slid into my car, wiped my face, and headed back to my hometown.

19
"Home"

It wasn't a lie.

As I stood by her bed and stared at her, that was the only thought running through my head. I'd spoken with her doctor and he'd even confirmed it. She'd had a stroke, a massive one that left one side of her body paralyzed. Her speech was slurred, too, according to Dan. And as she lay there in that hospital bed, sleeping peacefully, I was deluged with guilt. Had I upset her, worried her to the point of having a stroke? In my mind, I answered my own question with a resounding *yes*. I had done this. I was responsible. By running, not staying in touch, and openly defying the one person who'd always had my back, I had ruined her life. She would never be the same because of me and my selfishness.

I forced myself not to cry as I stood there next to my brother-in-law, and the first thing I did once the nurse informed me that the ICU visiting period was over was to rush through the hospital, into the elevator, and outside where I could breathe again. The weight of the truth of my sister's condition was stifling. I was surprised I didn't pass out in her room.

Dan, who despite being a carbon copy of Wade, was a good man, followed me, asked if I was okay. I nodded, pulled out my cell, and as he walked back into the hospital, I dialed the number to Hyacinth Manor.

"Hello?" Ms. Rosa answered.

"M-Ms. Rosa, this is LaVonda Ingram, is—"

"He's right here, sugar."

"Hey, baby," August said seconds later.

"Hey," I replied weakly.

"How is she?"

"Bad—paralyzed. And it's all my fault."

"Don't do that to yourself, Von. You didn't make her have a stroke."

"Didn't I? I worried her, ran away when she thought I was still mentally unstable, and maybe I was or am. I don't even know anymore."

"Von, you're the sanest person I know. Stop this. You are not to blame. You don't know what went on inside your sister's body or how long it's been going on."

"I shouldn't have worried her. I shouldn't have left like that. I should've called more."

"You shouldn't have met me? We shouldn't have been together?"

I shook my head. "I'm not saying that. I'm very thankful for you—I don't know what I'm saying. I can't think. I'm so tired..."

"Look, get some rest and call me later. I love you. Please don't let anything make you forget that. I love you and I'm waiting for you to come back home to me."

"I love you, too... *so much*."

***

I spent the next three days camped out in the ICU waiting area, visited Evetta as much as I was allowed, called August every day, missed him more with every second. During our visits, if Evetta was awake, we would talk. It was hard to understand her at first, but I eventually learned to decipher her speech. She was very happy to see me each time, as if she expected me to disappear at any moment. If she was asleep, I'd just sit by her bed and hold her hand and pray for her.

I tried to shake the guilt but couldn't, and the pressure of that guilt affected me greatly. By the time Evetta was moved from ICU to a regular room, I was so drained I could barely stand to be in the hospital, so I started sleeping in my house at night. But I couldn't really sleep when I was there because I was filled with anxiety about being away from the hospital, so I was out of it by the morning time from spending the night tossing and turning. I was too tired to call August every day like I had at first, yet more than anything, I needed to hear his voice. I missed him in my soul. I missed Hyacinth Manor. I missed his cabin. I missed being happy.

Anxiety—guilt—fear—depression were all I came to know. As a matter of fact, we became very intimate friends.

By the time she was discharged home, I'd been back in town a mere three weeks, had already lost close to twenty pounds, and I was having headaches on a daily basis. I'd moved into Evetta's and Dan's guest room but was only sleeping a couple of hours every night. I cooked her soft diet meals, helped her bathe and use the toilet, sat with her the entire time Dan was at work. I apologized a million times and even with all of that, the feeling of guilt wouldn't release its stranglehold on me.

20
"I'm Going Down"

There are stages to depression, sort of like individual stairs on a staircase. You start out walking down the stairs with ease. Your steps are sure and steady, but with each step, your legs weaken or your knees may buckle, or maybe you trip and fall part of the way down. Then things get successively worse—the light bulb hanging over the staircase goes out, a step begins to loosen, and one day you try to take a step only to find that your once sturdy staircase is now a slide, a slippery one, and the next thing you know you're sliding down into a pit of darkness that you eventually can't claw your way out of. You try to stop sliding, but you can't. You can't get off and eventually, you just wish it would end, all of it. Your life included.

Unbeknownst to me, I made the first step down the staircase of depression the day I returned to my hometown. Seeing Evetta was the next step, giving in to the feelings of guilt was akin to hopping over half of the steps on the staircase, but the day I called to find that August had left Hyacinth Manor was the day I stumbled onto the slide, *head first*.

"He's gone, sugar. Been gone for about a week now. He hung around waiting for you to call and I guess he just gave up," Ms. Rosa said delicately.

How long had it been since my last call? Two weeks? Three? I honestly couldn't remember. I was losing track of time along with the sanity I had managed to acquire at Hyacinth Manor. He must've thought I'd forgotten him, but how could he ever think something like that? "Well, did he say where he was going or when he'd be back?"

"No, honey, he didn't. He just… left."

I groaned softly. "I messed up coming here. I shouldn't have come. I'm so lost here," I said without realizing I'd said it aloud.

"Come on back then, sugar. You're more than welcome. Always will be."

"But August isn't there. I can't come back if he's not there. I messed everything up with him. He was the best thing I've ever had and I messed it up," I sobbed into the phone.

"Von, sugar—"

"And after all you did to put us together, putting me in that room and everything. I'm so sorry, Ms. Rosa."

"Sugar, what happened between you and that boy was all God's work, and what He puts together *no one* can separate. That room is a created thing; the power of love is in God's hands and His alone. Putting you in that room would've meant nothing had God not put you two on this Earth for each other. I've never seen anything like what you two have with each other. You come on back home, sugar, and I guarantee August will come back, too. You two are like magnets to each other, two halves of a whole."

I sniffled, heard Evetta call my name. "I've gotta go. If he comes back…"

"I'll tell him you called. And Von, remember what I said. You can always come back here. You have a standing invitation."

"Yes, ma'am. Thank you."

***

After learning that the love of my life had given up on me, I became enveloped in darkness and couldn't seem to find my way back into the light. I stopped sleeping altogether, barely ate, and my headaches became so severe that for a while I thought *I* was having a stroke. So I went to my family doctor, was prescribed sleeping pills and pain medication, and spent most of my waking hours popping pills when I wasn't waiting on Evetta hand and foot. Things began to blur for me, and I wondered why she couldn't see what condition I was in. Or was it that she could see it but just didn't care? She was happy, satisfied with my presence, would chatter on about how glad she was that I was there. But couldn't she see that I was dying inside?

I don't remember much of that time other than the perpetual numbness the medications induced. And then they stopped having their effects, so I started doubling doses. The last thing I remember about that period of time is driving to my house one day to check on things. I remember pulling into the driveway and putting the car in park. But I don't remember anything else about that day.

21
"You Can't See for Lookin'"

My eyes hurt like hell when I opened them, and I had the very definition of a splitting headache. It felt as if my skull was literally squeezing my brain, strangling it. I opened my cottony mouth and quickly closed it, smacking my lips in an attempt to drum up some moisture. I tried to adjust myself in bed, groaned in response to the pinpricks in my legs and the soreness in my hands. It was as if I'd been in an accident with a semi and the semi had won. "Water," I whispered, though I was sure I was alone.

"Von... Von, did you say something?"

Not only was I a physical wreck for some unknown reason, but my mental stability was in question because I could've sworn the voice belonged to August. But how could that be possible? How would he have found me here of all places, because from the smell of things, I was sure I was in a hospital... but why? "What happened?" I asked the person who sounded like August.

His face came into view. Whoever this guy was, he resembled August, but his beard was trimmed and his hair had been cut into a neat, low-cut fade. He was handsome, but he wasn't my August. "You OD'd, baby," he said.

"What—how?"

"I found you slumped over in your car in your driveway and called 911. They had to pump your stomach. I... I almost lost you." I could see tears pooled in his eyes.

I frowned as the throbbing in my head intensified. "I don't understand."

"I should've talked you into staying, but I thought letting you go was the right thing."

"I... I…" My eyes grew too heavy to hold open and the image of the false August became a messy blur.

And then I was engulfed in darkness.

***

It was as if my eyes were stitched closed. As hard as I tried, I couldn't open them. I couldn't move my mouth, either, but I could hear. I could hear someone praying for me, asking me to forgive them, asking God to help me. I heard the doctor say I needed rest. I felt the nurses check my blood pressure. I wanted to cry and scream and let them know I was still in here, but I couldn't. I hurt so badly, inside and out. Death would've been better than this.

So I prayed to die.

***

I finally woke up, I mean *really* woke up. My mind was clear, no headaches or body aches, and I realized the clean-shaven man really was August, *my* August—just a less rugged version of him. There he sat by my bed in a polo shirt and jeans, asleep. "August," I said in a raspy voice that startled me a bit.

He stirred a little, kept sleeping.

"August," I repeated.

He jerked to attention, fixed his eyes on me. "Von? You're awake?"

I nodded. "How long have I been in here?"

He stood and moved to the side of the bed. "A week."

"What… what are you doing here?"

"I came for you, baby. I was scared, wasn't sure I was ready to enter civilization again, but I had to for you."

My eyes filled with tears. "You came for me? How'd you find me?"

"Used Ms. Rosa's computer to Google you. Found your address."

"But... why?"

He gave me a look that was a combination of shock and confusion. "Why? Because I love you, baby. You came to me once, so I decided it was my turn to come to you. I bought a car, even bought myself a phone." He dug a cell phone out of his pocket and showed it to me. "I came to take you home."

"August..."

"I came to your house, found you in your car. I thought you were gone. You scared me, Von. What were you thinking?"

"I... I don't know. I wasn't trying to hurt myself. I was actually trying to stop the pain; I was hurting all the time. I've been so miserable here, miserable without you."

He shook his head, leaned in, and kissed my cheek. "I'm so sorry. At the very least, I should've come with you."

"It's not your fault. Everything is *my* fault. I always mess things up. I never do anything right."

"Who told you that? Your sister? Baby, you can't believe that."

"But it's true," I said through tears.

"No. It's. Not. As far as I'm concerned, you're perfect." He wrapped his arms around me. "I'm taking you home," he said into my ear. "You'll be better once I get you back home."

"I'm in a hole, August, and I can't get out of it. I *can't*…"

He tightened his hold on me. "Yes, you can! With God, you can. With me, you can."

"I didn't want you to ever see me like this. You shouldn't be here. I'm so ashamed…"

"Von, God put us together for a reason. You ever stop to think that I'm supposed to see you like this, to help you through this? To *love* you through this? Let me be here for you, baby. Let me help you."

I held onto him for dear life and nodded against his chest. "Okay."

He never left my side, prayed with me every day, helped me to the bathroom when I needed him to, helped me bathe and dress and though I was ashamed of what the rapid weight loss had done to my figure—sagging skin to go along with age-induced sagging breasts—he told me I was beautiful, no matter my size. When it was time for me to go home, he had my prescriptions filled for my antidepressants and did some research and made me follow-up appointments with a psychologist and a psychiatrist near Hyacinth Valley. For all of the "taking care of me" my sister and Wade boasted about throughout the years, I realized that August was the first person to truly know what that meant. When I would fall into a depression, neither Wade nor Evetta seemed very concerned because I always put on a happy face in public and that was the only thing that mattered to either of them—that I didn't embarrass them. And they certainly weren't hands-on when it came to me seeking treatment. As a matter of fact, until my most recent breakdown, Evetta was vehemently against me ever seeking treatment. Her advice to me was always to "suck it up."

We were to spend a couple of nights at my old house and then head back to Hyacinth Valley.

Our last night in my house, he held me close and asked me, "How do you feel, baby?"

"Better," I said.

"Good. Once we get home and you leave all of this behind you, you'll be back to normal. I'm gonna make sure of that."

In the early morning hours, I found myself awake, my mind full of thoughts that wouldn't let me rest. I thought and thought and thought until I conjured up the guilt I'd been battling, and since I was somewhere near the bottom of the upward swing out of depression but nowhere near completely out of the woods, I was powerless to fight it—the guilt. My need to atone became overwhelming. So on the day I was to leave with August, I snuck past him as he slept soundly on my sofa and went back to my sister's house.

22
"After the Pain"

"Where the hell have you been?!" my sister slurred as I entered her room that morning. "It's been days since you've been here! Dan couldn't get in touch with you and had to take off work to help me!"

As I sat down in a chair in her room, I numbly said, "I haven't been feeling well. I was in the hospital."

"Really?" she said as she lifted her right arm with her left hand and then let it flop lifelessly onto the bed. "Well, I haven't been feeling well, either!"

"I'm sorry."

"Yeah, you always are. You were sorry when we were kids and you'd spill something or scatter your toys about. Sorry when you made that C in 11th grade English, sorry when you dropped out of college."

"I dropped out of college because Wade wanted me to."

"Leave it to you to blame a dead man!"

"Evetta—"

"And you were so sorry when you worried me into this stroke. Well, sorry is not enough. I'll never host another dinner party or attend another charity event. I'll be stuck in this bed for the rest of my life, thanks to you."

"The doctor said physical therapy might help if you stop refusing it."

"*Might* help? Oh, just shut up and go get me some tea. And for

God's sake, don't forget the lemon."

I nodded and left to do as she commanded, her angry voice trailing me through the house. I passed Dan in the living room, nodded a greeting to him as I made my way to the kitchen. I mindlessly filled the kettle with water, placed it on the stove, then leaned against the counter and rubbed my newly throbbing head. This had been the routine since I'd returned to town to see about her. In her waking hours, if she was in a bad mood (which was most always), she'd berate me to no end. The problem was, I just took it because I believed I deserved it.

"Von," Dan said just as I was lifting the whistling kettle from the surface element.

Startled, I set it on the counter and turned to face him. "I didn't hear you come in."

"Sorry about that but there's something I need to say to you."

With a furrowed brow, I said, "Okay?"

"I used to always tell Wade he got the good sister. I'd tease him by telling him if I'd met you before I met Evetta, I would've married you instead. Our marriages were mismatched."

I wasn't sure if I liked where this conversation was going. "Um... Dan—"

"Wait, let me finish. I know Evetta is not the nicest person, but I love her, always will. I try not to get in you two's business because I know your bond is strong as sisters, but I need to say this: I have never liked how she treats you, how she's *always* treated you. What she did in taking care of you was extraordinary, but you don't owe her your life. I know you feel you need to repay her, but you've already done that by becoming a wonderful person, a much better person than she is."

"Dan—"

"And there's something else..." He lowered his head and shook it.

"What is it?" I asked softly, half-afraid to hear what he had to say.

"You are not to blame for her stroke. Evetta's had high blood pressure for years but has refused to take her meds, been trying different herbal supplements and alternative medicine but none of it has worked. Her doctor warned her that this would happen, but she wouldn't listen."

I shook my head in disbelief. "She never listens to anyone but herself," I mumbled.

He moved closer to me and placed his hands on my shoulders like his brother, my late husband, would sometimes do when he really wanted me to hear what he had to say. "You spent a lot of years with my rotten brother, and I know your childhood wasn't the best, and you deserve to be happy now. Von, I love you like the sister you are to me and I can't stand to see you in misery like this. Live the rest of your life for you. Leave today, *right now.* Evetta is my responsibility, not yours. Your responsibility is to live your life."

"But..."

"No buts. *Leave.* Go back to that guy who made you so happy. You had a light in your eyes that I've never seen before when you were with him. The light is gone now, Von."

I nodded, fought back tears. "Thank you for telling me all of this.

I really needed to hear it."

"I know, and that's why I told you. I was waiting for Evetta to tell you the truth, but she's too satisfied with feeding off of your guilt. She loves you, Von, but she loves you in a selfish way. You love her in a selfless way. That's not a healthy combination."

"I know." I sighed. "I was supposed to leave with August today. I was supposed to be on the road right now."

"Where is he?"

"If he's not asleep at my house, he's probably already gone."

"Then go get your stuff and go after him. He loves you. I could see that when I saw him back in Hyacinth Valley; it was written all over him."

I gave Dan a smile and hugged him for the first time in a long time. "Thank you so much."

"No problem."

I made Evetta's tea, added thickener to it per doctor's orders, and took it to her room, setting it on her bedside table. Then I went into the guest room and sat on the bed, Dan's words echoing in my mind, and when they stopped replaying, August's words took their place—*"Love is the only good reason to do anything, Von."* I loved Evetta, but what was compelling me to be there and to help her was guilt, not love.

I slowly gathered my things, now sure that it was right to leave, but still apprehensive about confronting Evetta. Once I was all set, I uttered a prayer for strength and returned to her room and said, "Um, Evetta?"

She glanced at me where I stood in the doorway and said, "Oh, good. I thought you'd snuck off or something. I'm thinking I want some tuna salad for lunch. You might have to run to the store for some mayonnaise, and make sure you put plenty of sweet pickles in it. I wonder if we have any of those club crackers in there. I know I'm only supposed to eat soft food, but screw that."

"Evetta, I'm leaving now so I won't be making lunch," I said softly.

She rolled her eyes and mockingly said, "What? Don't tell me you're *sick* again. When will you be back?"

"I won't be back."

She shook her head. "Running back to that mountain man? Gonna let him run through your money?"

I tilted my head to the side. "No," I said calmly, a newfound resolve building inside of me. "He has plenty of money, but I wouldn't care if he really was poor. I love you, Evetta, and I'm grateful for everything you've ever done for me, even the things I didn't and don't agree with, but I love that man with everything in me and I really don't care what you think about it or him."

"Wow, all it takes for you to forget what really matters is a handsome face and a roll in the hay, huh?"

I sighed as I set my bags on the floor outside her room and approached her bed. "Evetta, what really matters is God and love. And for all you taught me through the years, *August* taught me that. I can never repay what you did for me. All I can do is be a good person and live a good life."

She frowned and slammed her good fist against the bed. "Well, you can't leave. I don't care what you say, you owe me! After everything I did for you, you owe me! You're the reason I never had kids! I sacrificed everything for you! And being a good person and living in abject poverty with that man just will not do!"

"No, Evetta, you never had kids because Mama advised you not to, told you kids bring nothing but misery. I heard her say it and now that I think about it, that's probably why I never had kids, either. That, and I couldn't bear the thought of bringing kids into my horrible marriage. But none of that matters right now. All that matters is that I know the truth. I know I didn't cause your stroke any more than I made you take care of me all those years. I appreciate it, but I was Mama's responsibility, not yours, and she was wrong to put me off on you. And, Evetta, you're Dan's responsibility, not mine.

"And I want to apologize for blaming you for the way Wade treated me. I made the decision to marry him and stay with him, not you." I bent over the bed and kissed her forehead. "I guess I've said all I need to say. You might never speak to me again, and that's fine. But I love you, and I'm leaving now. Goodbye, Evetta."

"It'll never work! You're weak! You needed someone like Wade and you needed me. You need someone to think for you. You will never make it. That man can't take care of you!"

I turned and left the room without another word.

"Von! Von, you come back here! Von! Von!" she called after me but I ignored her, said goodbye to Dan, and as soon as I opened the front door, was met with a sight that melted my heart. August was in the driveway leaning against his new car.

"You found me again."

"Googled your sister's address, too."

"I guess next time it'll be my turn."

He walked toward me with a smile on his face. "Won't be a next time. I'm not letting you out of my sight ever again. You ready to go home, baby?"

I dropped my bags, fell into his arms, and said, "Yes."

23
"Booga Bear"

Some things are truly worth waiting for, like Christmases, birthdays, homemade ice cream, and much-needed vacations. Now I could add "making love to August Donovan" to that list. As I lay in the canopied bed inside our honeymoon bungalow, I wanted to pinch myself. Could anything in the world be as good as what I'd just experienced with August? And to think, I would have the pleasure of spending the rest of my life making love with and to him.

I tried to catch my breath as I glanced over at him. He was lying on his back with his eyes closed and a smile on his face. "What are you smiling at?" I asked.

His smile widened. "Oh, just thinking about how I put it on you."

"Wow, you're not conceited at all."

"Am I lying?"

I begrudgingly said, "No."

He laughed as he opened his eyes and looked at me. "Don't pout."

"I'm not pouting."

He rolled over and kissed me. "Yes, you are. What do I have to do to fix that?"

I shrugged. "I don't know... I guess you'll have to figure something out. Maybe you could, um, put it on me again."

"Oh, really? You want me to do that?"

"Mm-hmm."

"You know, if we keep this up, the only part of the island we'll see is this bed."

"I can live with that."

He reached over to the bedside table and grabbed his cell phone.

"Who are you calling right now?" I asked, exasperated. I was really ready for him to put it on me again.

"I'm not calling anyone, just setting the mood. I got an iTunes account and downloaded this song just for you."

I smiled when I heard Bobby Rush's "Booga Bear" begin to pour from the phone's tiny speakers. "Um, what are you trying to say?"

"That I thought you had a *booga bear* under there… and I was right."

"You're silly," I said through a laugh.

He rolled over onto his back and pulled me on top of him. "I know, but for the record, you put it on me, too, Mrs. Donovan. You really did."

I leaned over and kissed him gingerly. "Oh, I know, and you ain't seen nothing yet."

A warning to all of my Christian readers: DO NOT listen to "Booga Bear" or "Sue." (wink)

For tips on dealing with depression, visit:
http://www.helpguide.org/articles/depression/dealing-with-depression.htm

To locate a depression support group, visit:
http://www.dbsalliance.org/site/PageServer?pagename=peer_support_group_locator

For more information about Adrienne Thompson, visit:
http://adriennethompsonwrites.webs.com

Sign up for Adrienne's newsletter here:
http://eepurl.com/jnDmH

Follow Adrienne on Twitter!
https://twitter.com/A_H_Thompson

Like Adrienne on Facebook!
https://www.facebook.com/AdrienneThompsonWrites

Join Adrienne's Facebook group!!
https://www.facebook.com/groups/674088779363625/

Follow Adrienne on Pinterest!
http://www.pinterest.com/ahthompsn/

Connect with Adrienne on Goodreads!

https://www.goodreads.com/author/show/5051327.Adrienne_
Thompson

Also by Adrienne Thompson

The *Bluesday* Series:
Bluesday
Lovely Blues
Blues In The Key Of B
Locked out of Heaven (Tomeka's Story – A Bluesday Continuation)

The *Been So Long* Series:
Rapture (A Been So Long Prequel)
If (Wasif's Story) A Been So Long Prequel
Been So Long
Little Sister (Cleo's Story—a companion novel to Been So Long)
Been So Long 2 (Body and Soul)
Been So Long III (Whatever It Takes)
SEPTEMBER (The Christina Dandridge Story—a Been So Long companion novel)

The *Your Love Is King* Series:
Your Love Is King
Better

The *Ain't Nobody* Series:
Sedução (Seduction)—an Ain't Nobody Prequel
Ain't Nobody

Stand-alone novels:

Home

See Me

When You've Been Blessed (Feels Like Heaven)

Summertime (A Novella)

Nonfiction Titles:

Just Between Us (Inspiring Stories by Women) –as a contributor

Seven Days of Change (A Flash Devotional)

Poetry:

Poetry from the Soul… for the Soul, Volume II

All books are available at amazon.com, barnesandnoble.com, and kobobooks.com

**Please enjoy this excerpt from *No Pain, No Gain* (Latter Rain Series, Book 2)
– coming February 2016:**

Rochelle

I was so tired of sleeping alone I could scream. I mean, I talked a good game about how the last thing I wanted was the trouble of having a man, but truthfully, being a single mother was for the birds. Don't get me wrong, I loved my son and I loved being his mother when he was in his right mind. But any woman who says she'd prefer to do it alone is either lying or a straight-up fool in my opinion. What woman in her right mind would actually prefer to make every single decision and pay every bill and sign every note and attend every school function... alone? Not me, not really. There had been so many times in the past fifteen years that I wished someone could take up some of the slack for me, make one or two of the decisions, write a check, pick up some take-out—something! But I was alone in this, had been alone since the day he was born. Hell, his daddy wasn't even around for the birth.

Now, I'd never been a complete fool. Yes, I fell in love with a deadbeat, but I also made sure he took care of what was his, so I'd been getting child support all those years. We lived comfortably, and if I really wanted to, I could've quit my job. But what would be worse than sleeping alone would be spending every day—day in and day out—alone in my house. I would've rather worked somewhere, *anywhere*, than stayed in that house alone day in and day out. So I worked, took care of my son, went to church, cooked meals, and climbed into my bed... alone.

And I was so tired of it.

Okay, I guess I need to admit that my being alone was kind of my fault. At fifty, I still had a good body and face, and plenty of men in my backwater hometown had hit on me, some single and some definitely not single. But I just wasn't attracted to any of them—not one. I had a type and none of them fit my type. But then again, the one man who *did* fit my type got me pregnant and dumped me as soon as I told him because he wasn't "ready." Hell, neither was I, but I *got* ready because that's what grown folks do. They see a responsibility in front of them and they deal with it, not run away from it. Well, my Jesse Owens-like baby daddy took off and didn't look back.

Low down, dirty...

Oh, how I hated that man! Anyway, I knew I needed to figure something out. I needed to lower my standards or something. I needed and wanted a man. I just had no idea what to do about it.